MW01221923

WHISLING ISLAND WEDDINGS

A WHISLING ISLAND NOVEL

JULIA CLEMENS

PICKLED PLUM PUBLISHING

CHAPTER ONE

———————

DELICIOUS HINTS of gardenia and jasmine hit Bess's nose, followed by the unmistakable savoriness of roasted lamb—some of her favorite smells in the world. She could hardly believe this room she was sitting in would be part of her new home come evening. It was maybe a little old fashioned of them, but she and Dax had decided to live apart until their wedding night. The idea that not only this beautiful home but all of Dax would be hers this evening caused Bess's stomach to flip with excitement. All she had to do was get through her wedding, and this life with Dax that she'd been dreaming of would all be hers.

She smiled at her silly thoughts that reminded her of the words of a gameshow host, but it was truly how she felt. Sure, she was thrilled to be getting married. But honestly, the wedding—although it was going to be incredible thanks to her sister, Gen, and her best friend, Deb—was just the means to an end. The end being the start of her new life with Dax. Something she'd been waiting for for three years now. Heck, she'd probably been waiting for him all her life and just hadn't realized it. She'd never regret her marriage to Jon—her three incredible children were the result of that stable, loving union that only fell apart at the end—but she was so grateful to be right where she was today. She felt incredibly blessed to be able to feel this way.

"Oh my goodness."

Bess turned as she heard the voice of her one and only daughter, Lindsey.

"Mom," Lindsey gasped as she walked to where her mom sat in front of the vanity Dax had given her as a wedding gift. Bess had felt the gift highly unnecessary. Marrying Dax was gift enough. But the man loved to spoil her, and Bess wasn't about to complain.

Lindsey took both of Bess's hands and lifted her mother out of her seat. "I need the full picture," she said as her mother stood, and Lindsey took a step back.

Bess was pretty proud of her wedding dress choice. It had been difficult to find the right one, considering most brides were about thirty years her junior. But the simple, satin, cream dress with big bell sleeves and a deep but tasteful V-neck was better than Bess could've dreamed up for herself. The tiny little train gave the dress a bridal feel without being over the top. Her hair was pulled back into a simple French twist, and some of the jasmine that was decorating the main space of the home had been slipped into her hair by her hairdresser sister, Gen. The natural makeup that Gen had helped her apply might not be every bride's cup of tea, but it was definitely right for Bess.

"You look so so beautiful," Lindsey said as tears began to fill her eyes.

"Don't you start," Bess warned, causing Lindsey to laugh.

Five years earlier, Bess would've never imagined this scene was what her future would hold. She had totally dreamed of Lindsey's wedding day, getting to walk into the dressing room after her daughter had gotten ready to celebrate finding her forever love. But her grown daughter gushing over her at such a time? It seemed unnatural . . . and yet so perfect.

"I can't help it," Lindsey exclaimed. "I'm just so happy for you, Mom."

Bess nodded, knowing it was the truth. Lindsey had been a fan of Bess and Dax before there even was a Bess and Dax.

"You look pretty dang beautiful yourself, little miss," Bess said, suddenly recalling the nickname she'd had for her daughter years before and feeling the urge to use it.

Lindsey grinned as she did a quick spin to show off the floor-length, blush dress she wore. The front and back both had plunging Vs that were quite a bit deeper than the one Bess wore, but they were covered in a sheer material of the same blush color as the dress. The large slit that ran up the front of the dress wasn't something Bess would've chosen for her little girl, but the woman who stood in front of her wasn't her little girl anymore. Lindsey was a grown woman, older than Bess had been when she'd had her oldest child, and although the dress wasn't to Bess's taste, Lindsey looked gorgeous. She wore her long brown hair that was nearly the exact shade of chestnut as Bess's own in curls that flowed down her back.

"I know," Lindsey said confidently. "You should've seen the way Adrien's mouth dropped open when he came to pick me up." Lindsey laughed before adding, "It was almost as spectacular as the way my mouth dropped open when I saw my incredibly hot date in a tux for the first time."

Bess joined in with her daughter's laughter, loving that Lindsey was happy in her relationship. But Bess wished she wasn't picking up on the timidness Lindsey seemed to be having about taking her relationship any deeper than just casually dating the man of her dreams. According to Lindsey, Adrien was ready for the labels, the commitment and more, but she was skittish. Bess had a feeling that the unraveling of her own relationship with Lindsey's father had a lot to do with the fears Lindsey held. But Bess had gone to enough therapy to know Lindsey's fears were not Bess's fault, and all she could do was support her daughter in the best way she could. Bess just worried Lindsey would lose Adrien in the process, but thanks to the help of therapy, Bess knew that was up to Lindsey as well.

"I bet that was quite the sight to see," Bess said, and Lindsey fanned her face.

"You can say that again," Lindsey agreed.

Bess chuckled once again. Her daughter entertained her better than many comedians.

The door behind Lindsey opened, and a very harried-looking Deb peaked her head in before walking into the room and closing the door behind her.

"The rain is coming down harder," Deb proclaimed.

Bess nodded. She had a feeling the rain might disrupt her big day. She *had* planned an outdoor wedding on Whisling in October, after all.

"You're okay?" Deb asked as she ran her hand through her hair, a sure sign she was upset. But even a panicked and frustrated Deb was a put together, gorgeous Deb. The woman couldn't look bad, which was being proven right at that moment. Although her hands had to have run through her hair dozens of times, the wavy, auburn lob still looked like Deb had come straight from the hairdresser. Her simple, green wrap dress was perfect for not only running around in before the wedding but also for standing by Bess's side during the ceremony. Bess hadn't been sure she wanted to have bridesmaids—the idea seemed like one for younger women. But when she remembered the women who had had her back through thick and thin, she realized she didn't just want them at her wedding, she wanted them as part of this new beginning. So she had asked Gen, Lindsey, and Deb to stand with her on this very important day. Dax had asked his father, Levi (Gen's husband), and Dean (his sister Olivia's boyfriend), to do the same.

"Yeah, I mean it *is* October. Besides, we have a contingency plan," Bess said, reminding Deb that they'd gone through this very scenario. If there was too much rain that, even with the enormous white tent they'd set up, the outdoors would be too wet and muddy, they were going to have the main event in Dax and Bess's new living room. Since Dax's home was newly built, this could be a wedding and housewarming all in one. Bess loved being efficient.

"But you wanted the outdoors because your wedding with Jon was indoors," Deb lamented as she sat on the edge of the light blue comforter of Bess and Dax's new bed. They both loved blue, so the new home was filled with it. And even though most interior decorators would probably balk at the liberal use of the color, it made the house feel like home for Bess. There were touches that reminded her of the sea in every part of the place, lots of it thanks to Dax. He'd done most of the planning for their house, even though he'd asked Bess for opinions along the way. But she'd told him she trusted him, and honestly, the place couldn't have been more perfect for the two of them.

"I did. But it doesn't really matter that much today," Bess said honestly. Her first wedding had been over the top. Jon had wanted to shout from the rooftops that he was marrying Bess, and their guestlist had matched that goal. The church on Elliot Drive had been full to the brim, and Bess had worn the poofiest white dress her little eighties heart had desired. So when planning this wedding, she'd gone in the opposite direction. Not because she hated Jon that much—in fact, she'd invited him to the small affair today—but because that wedding had personified Jon and what he'd wanted. This day was about her and Dax. Simple and sweet. Their very own personification.

"You don't have to be so easygoing, you know," Lindsey said.

Deb nodded emphatically. "You're the bride. You get to whine, complain, and then demand your wishes be met," Deb added.

Bess grinned. She loved these two women with all her heart.

"Not sure mother nature cares too much about my wedding," Bess said.

Deb shook her head and groaned, "But she should."

"Yeah, she should," Lindsey added, now appearing to be highly amused by the situation. She'd known Deb most of her life and knew that when Deb got like this, it was best to lighten the situation.

"Are you mocking me, Lindsey Wilder?" Deb asked.

Lindsey's eyes went round with mock surprise. "Me?" She held her hands to her chest. "Never."

Deb chuckled and then breathed a sigh that sounded somewhat relieved. "You really don't care?" she asked.

Bess shook her head. "Really, truly," she said.

Deb nodded. "Well, then I guess I'd better get a move on. We're t-minus half an hour until you walk down that aisle," she said as she stood and walked to the door.

"Do you need any help?" Bess asked, standing up from her vanity.

Deb shot her best friend a look of pure horror. "You are the bride. You sit there and enjoy the day. All I'm going to do is issue a few commands to Luke. Then I'll be back and ready to do my duty as maid to the bride," Deb said, opening the door.

"You know that's not what you literally are," Bess shouted as Deb shut the door.

"Yes I am," Deb said loud enough for Bess and Lindsey to hear through the shut door, and both women fell into giggles.

Bess couldn't believe how relaxed she felt getting married this time compared to the overwhelming jitters she'd felt before walking down the long aisle of the chapel to Jon. Bess wasn't sure the reason. Maybe because this wedding would be so much smaller, maybe because she was older and wiser now. Or it could also be because doing anything with Dax just felt right. Whatever the reason, she was enjoying every moment of this day. And even though she was anxious to be Mrs. Dax Penn, she was also content spending the morning with her daughter as they sat in this lovely room, feeling beautiful in their pretty dresses.

"Does that mean you're my maid too?" Bess asked.

Lindsey nodded sagely. "Isn't that who I've always been to you, Mother?" Lindsey asked, and Bess would've thrown something at her daughter had a ball of paper or anything of the sort been within reach. But she settled for narrowing her eyes.

Lindsey burst into laughter and then fell into the gray armchair that sat near the vanity.

The door opened and closed again, this time revealing Gen. She looked stunning in her steel-colored dress, which offset her pale complexion perfectly. Hers was a wrap dress like Deb's, but it was floor-length. The bit of lace that covered the skirt made it feel a little more fancy than the simple cotton of Deb's dress. Bess had told her favorite women that their dress was up to them, and all three had declared Bess the best bride ever.

"I think Dax is more than ready," Gen said as she took the spot on the bed that Deb had vacated.

"What do you mean?" Bess asked, anxious that her soon-to-be husband was feeling the nerves she wasn't.

"He's already standing at the front of the living room where Deb is telling Luke to set up the archway of greenery you two will be married under," Gen said with a big teasing grin. "I told him the wedding was still half an hour away, but he just shook his head at me before standing up straight again. I think he's hoping if he stands there long enough, someone will grab you and the two of you can get on with this already," Gen added.

Bess grinned. That was pretty much exactly how she felt. The arch would be a nice touch, along with the flowers Gen and Lindsey had chosen at the florist and then painstakingly used to create lovely arrangements to decorate the ceremony space, but none of it felt necessary. As long as their guests arrived and they got married, Bess would be happy.

"So he's just waiting?" Bess felt a combination of adoration and worry for her cute fiancé.

"No. I sent him into the kitchen. Alexis was looking for a taste tester, and it seemed that was the only thing that could get Dax away from his spot in the living room," Gen said, causing all three women to laugh. Good food was the only thing that would compete for Dax's attention.

"Is Alexis overwhelmed?" Bess asked. Her coworker and friend had insisted on cooking the wedding luncheon all on her own. Bess had told Alexis that Winders would happily supplement whatever Alexis wanted to create, but Alexis insisted that the meal be completely made by her and her alone. And although Bess didn't doubt Alexis's ability—the woman was the best chef Bess knew—cooking a full meal for forty was a feat for a team of caterers. Alexis was one woman, and yet she'd insisted.

So they'd come up with a delicious, and Bess hoped fairly simple, meal of roasted lamb with mint jelly (Dax's favorite dish), baby golden mashed potatoes with thyme and rosemary, a Mediterranean salad full of roasted and fresh veggies, and Alexis's famous garlic rolls. Bess's mouth watered just thinking about the good food they would have following the ceremony, and she kind of felt like walking downstairs and standing in place, the way Dax had. She was ready to get this show on the road.

As Bess dreamed about food, a small clump of hair slipped out of her French twist, causing Gen to gasp and hurry to her sister's side to fix the error. Several minutes of primping later, Bess's hair was looking perfect again, according to Gen.

Deb burst into the room. "It's time," she said with all the flourish only Bess's dramatic best friend possessed.

"You all are marvelous," Bess said to Deb, her daughter and her sister. "Thank you for all you've done."

The day had come together only because of the labor and love those three women had put into every detail.

"You've done the same for each of us," Deb said, and Gen nodded.

"Not me," Lindsey pointed out.

Even as Bess laughed, she had to say, "Yeah. I just labored with you for twenty-two hours and then changed about two thousand diapers."

"I'm never going to live that down, am I?" Lindsey asked, and Bess stood, opening her arms in response.

Lindsey filled them, and then Bess felt more arms go around her as her sister and Deb joined the hug.

"Just be careful with Bess's hair," Gen warned from within the hug.

The sound of Canon in D drifted up the stairs, telling Bess it was finally time.

"Guys, I'm getting married," she said, suddenly feeling the overwhelming urge to cry.

"Nope. Nope, nope," Deb said as she ran back to the door to open it. "Get down there before you cry all that makeup off," the woman demanded.

Bess grinned. Thank goodness for these women.

Then she walked slowly to the door, careful not to trip on her train. It might've been small, but Bess was in three inch heels, so any train at all would be easy to trip over.

She looked behind her to see Gen bending over and

arranging the lovely bit of flowing fabric. Bess smiled gratefully at her sister who returned the gesture quickly.

"I am so happy for you," Gen said before Lindsey took Bess's arm and led her down the stairs.

The music filled Bess, making her grateful that they'd hired a pianist and cellist, even if for just these few moments. The live music made the moment all that much more real. Bess was getting married. Dax, the man who'd stood by her side through the thick and thin of the last few years, the hardest years of Bess's life, was downstairs. Ready to say *I do* and start forever with her. How did she get to this place? Whatever had brought her here was all worth it. Every tear, smile, pain and joy. Worth it.

Bess looked over to see a single tear slip down her daughter's cheek, and Bess blinked back her own emotion.

"These years . . ." Bess began as she and Lindsey got to the bottom of the stairs and joined her boys. Stephen and James were just as beautiful as their sister in their gray suits. They'd opted for the more casual route of suits, even though many of the other men in attendance wore tuxes. But the suits were just their style, and Bess was glad they hadn't gone the fancy route. Her boys looked perfect.

"They've been a little rough," Bess continued. "And I would not have made it without each of you." She met the eyes of Lindsey, James, and then Stephen. Each of her children beamed back at her, and Bess couldn't believe they were here. They'd been through the fire, their relationships had been refined, and now they were all so pleased for her. Bess smiled at the memory of the first time her boys had met Dax and their silly behavior in protecting their mother. But now Dax was part of their family. And this ceremony to cement that relationship was what they all wanted, not just Bess.

The first notes of *Can't Help Falling in Love*, the song she and Dax had heard on the radio the day of their engagement, began to play. Bess turned her attention to Deb and Dean, who would walk down the aisle first. The friends linked arms and shot back smiles toward Bess as they walked the short way from the hallway into the living room. Levi and Gen followed, Levi giving his gorgeous wife a kiss before they were out of Bess's sight. Then Dax's dad bowed to Lindsey, showing the young woman the kind of chivalry only a gentleman would, before they linked arms and walked out of Bess's view.

The music changed once again, and the soul stirring sounds of the Wedding March began. This was it.

Bess looked from Stephen to James, getting a kiss on either cheek from her sons, and then linked one arm with each boy. She stood in the middle of her handsome sons, feeling like the luckiest woman on earth as she walked toward the hallway that would lead them into the living room.

Bess's first steps into the room filled her sight with light, her eyes having to adjust from the darkness of the hall. Even though the day was overcast with rain, the floor to ceiling windows in their living room still allowed for a ton of light to flood the room. When Bess's eyes adjusted, she met the gazes of many of her guests. Olivia beamed and Alexis smirked. The place was full of the people she loved, and although it should've felt packed—the room, though quite large, wasn't made for forty wedding guests —it just felt cozy. Some people sat on her lovely, new blue couches while others were in the pretty, white folding chairs lined up in front of and behind the couches. And all of them were safe from the elements.

Flowers adorned every free space in the room, huge white vases with white flowers of every kind. Bess hadn't wanted to choose wedding colors, so Lindsey and Gen had decided to go with white flowers and lots of greenery. The result was breathtaking.

And then Bess could wait no longer. Her eyes went to the front of the room where she knew Dax would be waiting. Her strikingly attractive husband-to-be. The smile on his face said all Bess needed to see. He was as ready for this as she was, and she felt her boys trip as she sped up the pace. Bess just wanted to be with Dax.

A few chuckles escaped their guests, telling Bess her mad dash hadn't gone unnoticed, but she didn't care. She grinned as she took the final steps to the archway of greenery and her Dax.

"You are stunning," Dax breathed as if in awe of her.

But Bess couldn't imagine he could feel anywhere near as blessed as she did. She just shook her head, too overcome to speak, and Dax met her eyes. She and Dax could communicate with just a look.

At some point, she'd let go of her boys and now had her hands in Dax's. She wasn't sure when or how it had happened, but she'd found Dax and chosen to cling to him. A perfect metaphor for what she'd done in life. And now that she had him, she would never, ever let go.

The minister spoke beautiful words, but Bess was too giddy to digest much of what he was saying. When it came time for their vows, Bess had to focus. This was a once-in-a-lifetime moment that Bess wasn't going to miss.

"Bess," Dax began as his grip tightened on her hands. Bess gave his hands a squeeze, and he smiled before going on. "From the moment I met you, I knew you were someone special. You radiate a light from within that captivates all who know you. And I knew I wanted that light in my life every day."

Bess grinned, unable to show all she was feeling but hoping the small gesture would show Dax how much his words meant to her.

"So I chased you."

Everyone in attendance laughed, all of them close enough to know how relentless Dax had been in his pursuit of Bess.

"I thought I knew how special you were. But it was only after getting to know you that I began to realize how truly lucky I am. The closer I got, your light only grew. I began to not only crave you and that light, I knew I needed you. Yesterday, today, and forever. You are my love, my life, and my reason. My reason for being my best self. And I'm all too ready to say I *do*."

Dax's last words caused those in attendance to laugh, but the laughter wasn't as strong as the first bout since many had been choked up by Dax's previous words—Bess included.

"How am I supposed to follow that?" Bess asked when the minister asked her for her vows.

Their friends laughed with her, and Bess drew in a deep breath. "Life isn't always fair. For a long time, it felt like my downs overshadowed all my life's ups. But then you came along. And you outshined all of those downs. They were still there, but they no longer dragged me down. I was able to focus on the ups. Those never perfect but infinitely beautiful ups. And even though I know life's downs aren't over, each one will be better because I get to go through them with you," Bess said.

Dax whispered, "Forever," for her ears alone, causing her to choke up once again.

Bess cleared her throat. "I love you, Dax Penn. I promise today to choose us. To choose this. To work hard and to love even harder."

Bess felt her eyes well up with tears of overwhelming joy and knew her time was up. She couldn't say another word.

"I love you," Dax whispered, special words for her alone, once again. How could he make her feel so alive?

The minister finished the ceremony, and Bess and Dax finally kissed as husband and wife.

"Ahh!" Bess squealed after their kiss, unable to express all she was feeling with real words.

Dax laughed as he held her hand in the air, and the couple walked back down the makeshift aisle as a married couple.

Bess was married. She couldn't believe it. Losing the title of wife had been hard for her. She'd been unsure she'd ever find herself after that loss. But she had. And although the title was once again the most important one she held, she realized being a wife didn't define her. She was Bess Penn, a woman who held the titles of wife, mother, entrepreneur, cook, friend, aunt, sister, and so much more. In the time she'd spent alone, she'd found herself. Realized she liked herself. And it was only after knowing who she was that she'd been able to give her best self fully to another. So, with all of those titles and Dax by her side, Bess was ready to conquer the world. But then again, maybe she already had. So she'd do it again and again. Working hard and loving harder, just like she'd promised Dax.

CHAPTER TWO

JULIA WAS sure the smile on her face looked goofy, but never had she been more thrilled to see two people wed.

She had been to lots and lots of weddings throughout her life, but she'd never been more sure of a couple. Other weddings she'd been to had been full of grandeur: dresses that cost more than luxury cars and events that cost more than small homes. But there was something so real about this day. About those vows and this moment. Julia had never felt a love more real. And she wasn't even a part of it.

There was little in life Julia was envious of, but the moment Dax and Bess raised their clasped hands into the air, Julia realized she wanted that. Maybe even needed it. But where was a washed up, fifty-something starlet supposed to find love?

Julia shook her head. Well, it was good to dream. And maybe a dream was all this would ever amount to, but if she didn't at least hope for it, she had a feeling it would never come to pass. Her hope would give her dream a small chance.

The couple swept their way into the dining room where guests would mingle with them as the living room was converted from ceremony site to reception venue. The rain

⌐ to be letting up, so according to what Julia had over-
⌐b saying, the tables and chairs would be set up in the
⌐pace because it was the only place in the house large
enough to accommodate the five round tables that would seat
eight apiece. Julia had seen hardened wedding planners with
years of experience crumple under pressure much less than
what Deb was enduring, but the woman was a force. And fortunately, there was plenty of manpower available to see her vision
through.

Julia noticed Alexis scurrying to the kitchen, probably to
put the finishing touches on the food. Julia wanted to help but
realized it was safer for all involved if she stayed away from any
and all cooking.

So if she couldn't help there, Julia would stay in the living
room. Already, Luke and Wes, Deb's son, were pushing the
couches down the hall to who knew where. Deb was directing
Dean and Levi on where to place the huge flower arrangements,
and others were placing tables and moving the white chairs into
place around them.

Julia noticed Gen taking tablecloths out of a box and
decided that was where she could help.

"Let me," Julia said as she gathered the cloths from her
friend.

"You're a guest," Gen said as she tried to take them back.

"So are you," Julia said with a grin, nearly breathing a sigh of
relief when Gen let her take the job. Julia had come to realize
that only those who were true friends were allowed to bear the
burden like this. Allowing Julia to help meant she was really
part of this ramshackle family she'd made on Whisling.

Julia opened the first tablecloth and began to shake it out as
she walked toward a table that was already standing. She threw
the pristine white cloth over the round table and nearly got it to
the other side.

She was about to round the table when Ellis smirked from where he was finishing setting up another table and then walked her way.

"This looks like a two-person job," the country singing sensation drawled, and Julia bit the inside of her cheek to keep from melting at the sound: a mix of sexy and homey. How did he do it?

"I think I can manage," Julia said as she began to walk around the table again. But Ellis beat her to it and fixed the tablecloth so that it covered the table evenly.

"But it would be so much more pleasant to do it together, don't you think?" Ellis asked.

Julia shrugged. She knew it would be. The job would go much faster as well. She had a feeling this whole turnaround team was looking for speed. But the idea of spending more time with Ellis felt dangerous. She'd fallen for his charms at Bess and Dax's engagement party months before and then Ellis had left on his world tour, as he should have. And yet . . . Julia had been left on Whisling wanting more. It wasn't where Julia liked to be. Therefore, keeping a wide berth of Ellis seemed like the only option. Except, apparently, he wasn't going to make that easy.

Since it looked like Ellis wasn't going anywhere, Julia walked to the next table, threw one end of the tablecloth to Ellis, and then together they arranged it nicely. If he wanted to work with Julia, fine. But she didn't have to speak to him.

"I take it from this nonstop chatter that you missed me tremendously," Ellis drawled with that famous smirk of his, and Julia took a physical step back. She could already feel herself drawn in by his charms. But the man would be leaving. Maybe tonight. For months. Or maybe forever. Now that these wedding events were done, when would Ellis be back? He'd told Julia at the engagement party that he would be coming to the island after his tour, but who knew? Men like Ellis changed dime. And Julia didn't want to count on them. She count on him.

u got me," Julia deadpanned as they moved to the third table. Only two more to go. Then Ellis would go find his seat and Julia would go to her own.

Ellis chuckled as he caught the side of the tablecloth Julia threw at him, and they once again covered the table in unison. Even though it wasn't big, there was something satisfying about the job. Especially as Julia looked back and saw the covered tables being adorned with smaller versions of the flower arrangements that filled the huge vases in the room. She was the first step to the tables looking complete. And it felt good.

"Did I do something to offend you?" Ellis asked as they moved on to table four.

"Not at all," Julia said, concentrating on getting every wrinkle out before moving on to table five. She'd noticed Gen having to do that for them back at the first table, so she wanted to do a better job. Even if it meant a few more moments with Ellis.

"Really? Because you've hardly said a word to me," Ellis added.

Julia shook her head. "Just concentrating on the task at hand," she said as they finished covering the final table. Thank goodness. Now she could get drawn away by something urgent —there had to be other wedding jobs—and Ellis would enjoy his meal and then be on the next flight to who knew where.

"Covering tables can be quite strenuous." Julia could hear the laughter in his voice, but she was okay with being teased. It was better than being pulled into his realm. The place that made Julia feel . . . well, more than she wanted to feel.

"I like to be thorough with any job I'm given," Julia said matter-of-factly as she smoothed out the last of the wrinkles and then glanced up to see Deb making her way to the first table with an entire basket of silverware. That was Julia's way out.

"If you'll excuse me," Julia said, shooting Ellis her red-carpet smile before heading toward Deb.

"Do you need a hand?" Julia offered her friend who sighed with relief as soon as Julia spoke.

"Oh my goodness, could you?" Deb asked as she handed off the basket to Julia, wasting no time. "That way I can grab the plates and we should be all set."

"Of course," Julia said as she looked at the jumbled mess of silverware in the fabric-lined basket. As far as she could see, there were only forks, spoons, and knives. She figured dessert spoons would come when the dessert was served.

A pro at attending events where meals were served, Julia knew she could knock this job out of the park as well. And bonus, she'd lost Ellis somewhere along the way.

As Julia put out the first place setting on the napkin that had already been placed, she wondered if she'd been too abrupt with Ellis. After all, he hadn't done anything wrong. Had Julia hoped he might call her after the engagement party? Um, yup. But did that mean he should have? No. He'd made no promises. And yet, maybe that was the problem. It had felt like he had. The way he'd spoken to Julia made her feel like she was part of his world. But she wasn't. And the only way for her to be safe from falling into that same trap again was to avoid him. Especially on a day like today. One filled with an almost whimsical love that had Julia craving for something exactly like it.

The clearing of a throat caused Julia to look up.

She quickly fought the urge to close her eyes. Or to look back down and pretend Ellis wasn't there. But that was impossible. So instead she smiled.

"Looks like you could use some help?" he offered, and Julia

knew she couldn't say *no*. It would take her ages to do the job alone. With Ellis, it would move right along.

"Grab a handful of forks. You can follow me," Julia instructed.

Ellis smirked once again. "Yes ma'am," he said as he gave Julia a small tip of his imaginary cowboy hat before doing exactly as she'd asked.

"Heard you sold that screenplay of yours," Ellis said, and Julia nodded, filling with pride.

Part of her had wondered if the day would come where she'd be known for something other than her on-screen roles. Julia knew she was lucky to have had her career, but with the way it had felt cut short, she'd wanted more from life. And her screenplay had given that to her.

"I did," Julia responded as they finished up the first table. Man, this job went a lot slower than the tablecloths. Julia wasn't sure she'd be able to avoid falling into conversation with Ellis for the entire time. So she opted for safe topics. Like work.

"And your tour seems to be going well. Did you really sell out everywhere you played?" Julia asked, glancing at Ellis before realizing that was a bad idea. She'd heard about smolders before, even seen a few on her on-screen counterparts, but nothing Julia had ever seen before could've prepared her for the look Ellis was sending her way. So she did what any sane woman would do. She dropped her eyes to the basket and held onto that sight like the lifeline that it was.

"Have you been keeping tabs on me, Julia?" Ellis asked, and Julia swore she could *hear* the smolder. Was there no escaping it?

"If you call listening to the radio or watching the news keeping tabs on you, then yes, that's exactly what I've been doing," Julia said as she hurried through her task. She wanted to make sure the place settings looked nice, but she needed to get these utensils lined up quickly.

"I knew it," Ellis drawled. "You've missed me."

Julia didn't dare admit the truth, but she didn't want to lie. Why did the man have to be so confident? No other person Julia knew would make her admit to that outright. Especially when it was obvious she was pulling away from him. But no, of course Ellis couldn't be normal.

"With all my heart." Julia hoped she'd inserted just the right amount of sarcasm into her voice to throw Ellis off her scent. Why did setting out spoons and knives have to take so long? They finally moved on to the third table.

"I can take over this job if you're needed elsewhere," Julia offered, hoping against hope that Ellis was bored of what they were doing. Men like Ellis had short attention spans, didn't they?

"Nowhere else I need to be," Ellis said slowly before adding, "Nowhere else I'd rather be."

Julia felt her heart flip. Oh, the man was good.

So what to do now? Julia could keep fighting it, fighting Ellis. But look where that had gotten her. Or she could play along. Have a bit of control in this situation that felt a bit too topsy turvy for her.

Julia decided on option two.

"You talk a good talk, Ellis Rider. But the problem is, your walk has a little catching up to do," Julia said honestly, and she felt a genuine smile cover her face. Let Ellis try to decipher that one.

Julia could feel Ellis's eyes on her as they both continued their work. His gaze was unnerving, but she also felt incredible that she'd stunned him into silence. Julia set a spoon and knife at a place and then moved on to the next. They were now more than halfway done.

"Are you saying I'm all talk, Julia?" Ellis finally asked as they finished up table three.

Julia turned to meet Ellis's gaze, the one she'd felt on her for minutes now, but meeting it was a bad move. In engaging that sea of soulful brown, longing immediately washed over her.

What was she doing? She mentally shook her head because she couldn't physically do so. Not without Ellis realizing the effect he'd had on her.

Julia looked back down as soon as they arrived at table four and got to work.

"Something like that," Julia muttered, feeling a lot less confident about her words than she had before. Somehow, someway, even after Julia had felt like she'd been the one to win the game between them, she'd still come out flustered and unnerved.

Julia felt a big, warm hand grip her arm softly. She went still. Ellis's touch was like a more poignant version of his gaze, which caressed her while at the same time making each nerve ending of her body come to life.

Julia swallowed before looking up. She had to meet his eyes. She had a feeling Ellis wouldn't let go of her until she did, and his touch was making all kinds of messes in her mind. How did he do this to her? Julia had been touched in this same way by dozens, maybe even hundreds, of men. Between dates, her on-screen loves, and even just men showing her to her seat, the touch was really an innocent one. And yet . . .

Those milk chocolate depths were waiting for her when she finally looked Ellis in the eye. She'd never had a look make her crave so much. She had to look away. And yet she couldn't.

Ellis took a step closer. There were only inches between them. Julia froze.

"I would like to walk the walk, Julia," Ellis said before dropping his head to whisper in her ear. "Just tell me what you want."

Ellis's lips brushed Julia's ear, causing a riot of fluttering in her belly and beyond. Holy crow. Julia swallowed, willing herself not to look the way she felt. She placed a hand on the chair beside her to keep herself upright, worried that if she didn't, her knees would give out. The truth is, she would've swooned. If she hadn't held herself up, she would've swooned. Did women actually feel this way in real life? Julia had played characters who'd felt this kind of immediate, intense attraction, but reality didn't work like this, did it? She would've denied it forever, except that it was happening. To her. Right now. And she wasn't sure how to manage it.

Julia decided all she could do was ignore what Ellis had said. What he had done. That was the only way to concentrate on the task at hand and shield her heart. Because she had a feeling that if she opened any part of herself to Ellis, the rest of her would fall. And she couldn't do that. Not when the man would be leaving within hours.

Julia went back to placing spoons on the right and knives on the left. Her movements felt robotic, but it was all she could manage. Fighting the part of her that was screaming to give Ellis Rider a chance was a nearly impossible feat, but that voice had to be ignored.

Table four was done. Ellis, heaven bless him, had given her some space. She wondered if he knew the battle she was fighting. Or if he could see how much she was actually falling and it had freaked him out. Men like Ellis wanted women to adore them but never to love them. At least that had been Julia's experience. Because love had an expectation of being returned. Not that Julia loved Ellis. Far from it. At least while she was fighting the part of her that wanted to fall.

"What do you want from me?" Ellis asked softly as Julia began to set out the first spoon on table five. So much for giving her space.

Julia swallowed.

For you to tell me you'll be back. That this is more than a harmless flirtation. That you actually care. Those thoughts screamed at her, but Julia opted for a shrug. She wasn't sure she could trust her mouth once it opened.

"Do you want to know what I want from you?" Ellis asked as Julia continued setting out spoons and knives. Two more places and she'd be done.

Julia shook her head, concentrating more on getting her job done than on anything else. She had to get it done. Then she could walk away, find a seat between two of her friends, and Ellis would ride away into the night.

Ellis placed his hand on her arm once again, and Julia had to stop. She could only fight the part of her that wanted Ellis for so long.

"I want you to give us a chance," Ellis said softly.

Julia turned to him. He couldn't be serious, right? Flirting with her was just a game. A fun way to pass the time while he was at a buddy's wedding.

"A chance?" Julia asked, knowing she must sound like a simpleton. But she needed him to clarify.

"I like you, Julia. Not the woman from the big screen but you. This woman who I've gotten to know. You're funny and beautiful. You're smart as a whip. I hate weddings, and yet I was looking forward to today for the last couple of months because I knew I'd get to see you again. I was serious about coming to Whisling after my tour is done. I would love to really get to know you. But I have to say, I'm feeling mixed signals coming from you. Does my admission scare you?" he asked, and he dropped her hand, telling Julia the ball was now in her court. Ellis had laid it all out there. At least it seemed like he had. Was he serious?

Julia was afraid that he wasn't. That she was just a passing

fancy. Men had sometimes played the game of getting her attention, and when they'd succeeded, the game was over. They were
the winners and Julia was always, always the loser.

So it was up to Julia. Was Ellis worth the risk? Worth dropping her mask of indifference? Because he could be toying with
her. She would never know until she gave him a chance. And at
that point it would be too late. Once she found out, she would
be hurt. But then again, what if . . . what if Ellis was being
genuine? Julia knew she liked what she'd seen of Ellis. She
wanted to give him a chance. But she was just so scared.

Julia realized it was just the beginning of whatever was
happening between them and that most people wouldn't be so
guarded this early on. Ellis wasn't asking for forever. He just
wanted to get to know her. But Julia knew where she stood, and
she already felt so much for Ellis. If she gave him that opening
and he decided he'd won the game . . . where would that
leave her?

But Julia wasn't in the habit of letting fear be her guide. Did
she really want to start doing that now?

No. She didn't. She might get hurt but . . .

"I'm sorry about the mixed signals, but there are no mixed
feelings," Julia said, sounding a lot more confident than she felt.
"I like what I know of you, too."

"So you wouldn't mind spending the rest of the evening as
my date?" Ellis asked.

Julia shook her head. She was really doing this.

"Let me just talk to Gen and make sure we can get seated
together then," Ellis said with a grin, taking a few steps toward
where Gen was working as Julia remembered she still had a job
to do.

"Sounds good," Julia said softly, sounding as vulnerable as
she felt.

"Hey," Ellis said as he took a step back toward Julia. "I know you've been hurt, and I'm sorry that you have. But I can promise this. I mean what I say, and I say what I mean."

Julia nodded, feeling reassured. Ellis didn't have to do that. Her past hurts weren't up to him to fix. And yet he was trying to. Because he cared? Julia hoped so.

Ellis deleted any space between the two of them and then dropped a kiss on Julia's forehead, making her feel light.

"I'll be right back," he promised before sauntering toward Gen. Julia tore her gaze away from Ellis's retreating form and got back to work.

———

ELLIS WAS true to his word and was the epitome of a gentleman date all afternoon. Julia didn't open a single door or pull out any chairs. The man stayed by her side, and heaven knew that made Julia's heart swell...just a bit.

Julia noticed the looks Deb, Nora, Gen, Alexis, Olivia, and even Bess were shooting her, all wondering what the heck was going on. But because Ellis didn't leave her side, no explanations could happen. Julia had to admit, she wasn't all too disappointed about that. She just continued smiling, catching Deb mouthing, "All right, girl," at one point.

"You know, of all the men I know, Dax was probably the last I figured would find his match," Ellis said quietly as Dax and Bess began their first dance. Bess looked lovingly up at her husband, and Julia felt her heart clench. Mostly with joy at the expression of love, and maybe a tiny bit of jealousy.

"Really?" Julia asked, glancing to her side where Ellis had pulled his chair so that it was right beside hers. He had his strong arm slung around the back of her chair, and every so often he would tickle her bare arm, maybe Julia's favorite part of the evening thus far.

Ellis nodded. "The rest of us all sing about love—deep down I know we're all romantics—but Dax . . . he was always that tough businessman, you know?"

Julia grinned. She did know. The Dax now and the Dax before Bess were nearly two different men. Julia wasn't sure when Dax had first told her about Bess, but the man was a catch —all the women she knew were aware of that—so Julia had wondered what kind of woman had snagged the guy who everyone was interested in. Julia wasn't sure she'd approve of whoever that woman was. But then she'd met Bess. Found out that she was as genuine as people came. And Julia had loved the two of them together.

"Wait." Julia loved where their conversation had gone, but she had to back up a minute. "All of you who sing about love are romantics?" Julia couldn't help her teasing grin, but what Ellis had said had just been too darn cute.

Ellis shrugged. "Just waiting around for the right woman," he said, his deep voice carrying the words right to Julia's heart. Oh dear. She was in trouble.

Ellis suddenly stood, and Julia's bare shoulders felt cold with the absence of his arm.

Julia looked up to see Ellis offering her a hand. "Would you like to dance?" he asked.

Julia looked to the dance floor, aka the dining room, to see that it had been opened up to all the guests.

"I'd love to," she said as she took his hand and was pulled against his hard chest. She'd always wondered what was beneath all those Henleys, and heaven bless, his chest felt just as nice as she'd imagined.

Ellis moved away but kept ahold of Julia's hand as he led her across the living room to where most of the other couples in the room were already swaying together.

Can't Help Falling in Love, Bess and Dax's wedding song,

ended, and suddenly the crooning that came over the speakers was a voice Julia knew well. She looked up to see a slight redness come over Ellis's cheeks as he also recognized the voice.

Ellis shot a glare over Julia's head. She was guessing he was sending it in Dax's direction. She turned around to see Dax howling, and even Bess smiled at the change of song.

But Ellis didn't let them take his attention for long. Julia felt his big hands span her waist, and she turned back toward her date, winding her arms around his neck.

"For what it's worth, I love that we're dancing to your song," Julia said, smiling up at Ellis.

He returned the gesture. "Then I guess I won't have to pummel Dax before his wedding night."

Julia laughed as Ellis pulled her closer. She could get used to this.

As they swayed, Julia noticed Ellis humming along to the music.

"You can sing if you'd like," Julia offered, more for herself than for her date. Dancing with a man while he sang her *his* song? That would check about three things off her bucket list. The song was one of Ellis's older ones, but it was a favorite of Julia's.

Ellis began to sing the words softly, just loud enough for her to hear. His deep bass felt like it was humming along her skin.

"Did you write this one?" Julia asked when Ellis stopped singing. They were drawing the attention of other couples around them, and Ellis seemed to want to keep a low profile. It was like he didn't want to share Julia with the rest of the room. She felt the same way, so she was kind of grateful when he stopped. She hoped she'd get another chance to be serenaded soon. But hopefully next time it would be just the two of them.

Ellis nodded.

"I've written most of my songs. Definitely all the older stuff," he said. "I would like to write all of it, but I've been working so much recently. Another reason why Whisling is so appealing. I feel like I'd be inspired if I came back here." Ellis's eyes bore into Julia's soul, leaving her without any doubt of what, or rather who, that inspiration would be.

"Who was this one about?" Julia asked, feeling curious. The song was beautiful and relatable. A man wanting to wake to the same woman every morning, unable to believe his luck that she was his.

"I didn't know the woman then," Ellis said, tucking a stray curl behind Julia's ear. She swore that same one loved to come loose from any hairstyle she attempted. "But I'm pretty sure I know her now," he added.

Julia's stomach warmed. Oh, he was good.

"You do have a way with words," Julia said with a chuckle.

"Only when I truly mean them," Ellis responded.

Julia felt weak in the knees again. This man would be the death of her. Or at least a broken bone, if she wasn't careful.

Ellis seemed to realize that Julia was at a loss for words because he went on. "I still remember the first time I saw you. In that commercial for the diet soda," he said.

Julia shook her head. No one remembered her from that commercial. Her career hadn't truly started until a year later, with her first big movie.

"You do not," Julia said.

Ellis laughed, a deep sound that warmed her. "Are you saying I didn't see you?" he asked.

"I'm saying you can't remember that. No one remembers that. Except for those entertainment documentaries that talk about my life," Julia said.

Ellis shook his head. "I remember that commercial. You were wearing red shorts and a white t-shirt," he said. Then he added, "Your hair was still dark then."

It was. Julia had dyed her hair the ice blonde she was known for for her first role.

But Ellis must've just watched one of those documentaries, right?

"You took my breath away. I was writing some of the stuff for my first album, and I thought to myself, now there is a woman I could write a lifetime of music about."

"You did not," Julia said, shaking her head. She couldn't believe it.

"Swear on my favorite guitar," Ellis said, and Julia paused her swaying to look up at Ellis. He was serious.

"I met you three times before you remembered who I was," Ellis added.

Julia grimaced. "Really?" she asked.

Ellis chuckled. "It was before either of us were represented by Dax. I was a country nobody at those Hollywood parties you were the star of."

"But I didn't remember you?" Julia asked, feeling mortified. She hated that she'd been that person. But if she did want to justify her actions, that Julia Price had met handsome men at every event. Typically they all wanted something from her and were willing to give as little in return as possible. It had been safer for Julia to always keep a barrier up.

"Honestly, I didn't care. Getting to talk to you without the chance of you recalling the previous conversation gave me a bit more confidence," Ellis said.

Julia laughed. Of course he'd made it a positive. Ellis was like that. He was ease personified.

"So you forgive me?" she asked.

Ellis scrunched his eyebrows. "Maybe," he said, giving Julia an answer she wasn't expecting. "As long as you call me at least once a week when I go back on tour."

Julia felt her eyes widen. Ellis wanted to keep in contact after today? He'd said he was wanting more but . . .

"I guess I could do that," Julia said, schooling her features and playing way more hard to get than she was feeling.

"Then I guess I can forgive you," Ellis said with a wink.

Julia laughed. He knew she was playing, and he was content to play right back.

The music came to a close all too quickly as Dax went up to the front of the room.

"As much as I love you all, it's time for you to get out," Dax said, causing the crowd to laugh and his beautiful bride to blush.

The group slowly made their way toward the door, none of them wanting to anger their host. If he said it was time to get out, they'd all get out.

As Julia and Ellis walked out the front door, she noticed the sun was setting behind them. The red and orange light bathed the clearing sky, the dripping trees, and the departing guests. It really had been a perfect day.

"Where are you parked?" Ellis asked, and Julia pointed down the driveway to where she'd left her car.

Ellis put his hand on the small of her back, leading her in the direction of her car.

"I had a great time," Julia said honestly, feeling freer now that Ellis had asked her to keep in contact. She realized he'd done so much to show how much he liked her, but she really hadn't done much, thanks to her fears of appearing overeager.

"I did too," Ellis responded immediately. "So great, I'm honestly contemplating calling off the rest of my tour."

Julia spun to look at Ellis. He couldn't be serious.

When she saw that there was no trace of humor on his face, Julia knew she had to talk him out of it. Singers lost their entire careers for less than that.

"You can't," Julia said.

Ellis nodded forlornly. "I know. But that doesn't mean I don't want to," he said.

Julia sighed. She had to admit, a small part of her wished Ellis could call it off as well. They had the start of something special, but it felt like it could all be lost when he left the island. It couldn't be helped though.

"Where do you play next?" Julia asked, feeling a little melancholy that after that walk to her car, she wouldn't see Ellis for months.

"Omaha," Ellis said as Julia's heel got caught in the grass. Ellis grabbed ahold of her waist with one arm to keep her from falling and then didn't let go of her as they continued to walk again.

Julia's car was now only a few steps away. Was there a way to prolong this evening?

"Tomorrow?" Julia asked.

Ellis shook his head. "In three days."

Oh. He had a bit of a break.

"Do you fly out of Seattle tonight?" she asked, and Ellis nodded.

So much for that. Julia had hoped she'd have him for a little bit longer.

"At least I was supposed to. But . . . would you want to go to dinner? I'm sure I can get my assistant to change my flight."

Julia grinned. "I thought you'd never ask."

———

ELLIS FOLLOWED Julia to her house. She was planning on dropping her car off at home and then hopping in with Ellis so that they could go down to Elliot Drive to find a place for dinner. But it was only when Julia was alone in her car that she realized her feet were killing her. She really doubted Ellis would care if she took a few minutes to change into a new pair of foot torture devices. Why did women insist on heels getting higher and higher?

As Julia drove, she began to think about some of her favorite moments from the wedding when the touchscreen on her car's dashboard lit up. She looked down to see it was the caller ID of Avien Security. Why was her security company calling her at six on a Saturday evening? They typically only checked in when things went wrong.

Julia's worries began to mount as she answered the call.

"Hello? Ms. Price?" the voice on the other line said.

"This is she," Julia responded.

"This is Duke from Avien Security. I'm calling because it looks like there was a security breach at your home."

"A what?" Julia's voice cracked as she asked the question. She'd had a few security scares over the past couple of months, but they'd never amounted to anything. A security breach? That sounded serious.

"We see that you're away from the home?" Duke said, and Julia responded in the affirmative, even though he had yet to answer her question. She knew they already knew where she was because she had a tracker in her phone that the security company used. He was just asking the question as part of their routine. Most would balk at that kind of lack of privacy, but Julia had chosen her well-being over privacy. With the kind of work she did, it was often one or the other.

"Duke, you said a security breach?" Julia asked.

The security she had on her home was state of the art. Someone would've had to ram through her iron gate or scale over her twelve-foot walls. Which was it? And why were her hands beginning to sweat at just the thought? She knew the answer to the second question. It was because she knew what this meant. Someone had been determined to get into her home.

"I did, ma'am," Duke responded. "At just before eighteen hundred hours, a person we are now presuming to be a male scaled the walls in an area where the foliage is quite dense," Duke explained as Julia drove. Well, Julia was cutting down that tree or bush immediately.

"Wait, Duke, I'm on my way home now. Is it safe?" Julia asked, wondering if she should pull over. Ellis was following her, and the idea of getting out of her car and hearing this news with him sounded way better than what was happening.

"It's safe, ma'am," Duke replied, and Julia realized she should just press forward. Her home was only about a minute or so away. "As soon as the cameras picked up on the male climbing the wall, the protocol previously set forth by you and our company began. The police on the island were called along with a Mr. Dax Penn," Duke said.

"You called Dax?" Julia groaned. Of all the nights to interrupt her friend and manager. Hopefully the security company had called a work line for him that he wouldn't look at until he and Bess were well on their way to Tahiti for their honeymoon.

"Yes, ma'am. That is protocol," the man said, sounding just like a robot. She knew Avien hired the best of the best when it came to security, but they could work a little on bedside manner.

"So you called Dax and the cops. Are they at my home now?" Julia asked.

"The police are. We were unable to get ahold of Mr. Penn," Duke said.

Julia sighed. At least there was one relief in all of this.

"Please don't call Mr. Penn again," Julia requested.

"Noted, Ms. Price," Duke said. Then he continued, "The police are investigating and will stay until you return to the premises. Can we give the officers permission to enter your home?"

"Yes, of course. Whatever they need," Julia responded, and she heard typing on the other end of the call.

"We have a tech and security officer en route," Duke added after the typing ended.

"A what?" Julia asked. That was not part of the plan she'd set up with the company.

"If there is any sort of security breach, we send our tech out to fix what went wrong and a security officer to guard the premises until the threat has been neutralized."

"The threat hasn't been neutralized?" Julia asked, her voice squeaking. Now that they weren't just talking logistics, the fear that a person had broken into her home was back. Someone had invaded her safe space.

"I'm sure it would've been had we had an officer on site. The officer our company highly suggested," Duke repri- manded before his tone went neutral again. So maybe Duke wasn't this cold with every client. Julia seemed to have earned his ire because at the initial installation, she had declined the company's strong recommendation that she keep one of their men permanently on site. The result was that she'd made their job harder and made the company look bad in the process. Someone had broken into her home, and not only had Avien not stopped it, that someone had gotten away. Granted, it would've been hard for them to catch him considering the distance, but she could see that this kind of failure wouldn't sit well with any of them. Julia had briefly thought about sending the security officer away once he got to the island, but now there was no way she was going to do that. At least for the time being, she would do just as her security company advised.

"As far as how much of a threat we have, that is for the secu- rity officer to determine. Both the officer and the tech should arrive on Whisling Island by twenty-one hundred hours," Duke said. "Will there by anything more I can do for you, Ms. Price?" he asked.

"Do we know anything more about the person who broke in?" Julia asked as she pulled into her driveway. Sure enough, she had to maneuver around three police cars to park in her garage, and when she looked back at Ellis behind her, she saw his mouth open in shock. She would've called to warn him except that she was still on the phone with Duke.

"We have determined him to be male. Approximately six foot and two hundred pounds."

That size was not at all reassuring. Julia would be pulling her pistol out so that it would be beside her as she slept. She might be well trained in martial arts, but this man had a good eighty pounds on her. She wasn't cocky enough to think she could take on just anyone in a fight.

She realized Duke had stopped talking. "Anything else?" Julia asked.

"The man left you a rose," Duke said, causing a chill to run down Julia's spine. A rose?

"With a note," Duke added, and Julia fought the over-whelming fear that clawed at her. What had the note said?

"You will go over the note with the police on site. Is there anyone you can have stay with you until the officer and tech get to you? Protocol is for Mr. Penn to do so, but since he seems to be busy . . ."

Julia looked in her rearview mirror to see Ellis getting out of his car. Would he stay with her? That was a lot to ask of a man after their first sort-of date. If he wouldn't, she'd find someone else. She was sure Olivia and Dean would be all too happy to help, but Olivia had her girls. Maybe Gen and Levi. But they had their children as well. There was no way Julia would allow children to be part of this mess. She couldn't think of who she'd call just yet, but it would come to her.

"I'll be fine," Julia said, now just wanting to get off the call with Duke. She wanted to get inside, see the kind of damage that had been done, read that note. Julia shivered again, but she had to be tough. Whoever this was probably wanted her to fall apart. The last thing she was going to do was give a man who'd broken into her home what he wanted.

"Please call me if there is anything else you'll be needing, and I will call you again in an hour to check in," Duke said.

"Per protocol," Julia responded, remembering the plan.

"Yes, ma'am."

"Goodbye, Duke," Julia said, feeling a tiny bit of relief at getting off the phone. She knew she was probably being a bit too hard on Duke—the man was just doing his job—but Julia's frustration was mounting. And Duke, nearly a thousand miles away, seemed to be a good place to dump some of that.

Julia looked up at the sound of her car door opening. "Is everything alright?" Ellis asked.

Julia only had the strength to shake her head. She already felt so exhausted, and the ordeal was just beginning.

"Someone broke in," Julia said after she'd taken a fortifying breath.

"What?" Ellis asked as he looked back at the empty cop cars. Julia assumed they were walking around the premises, trying to figure out what had happened.

"Are you Ms. Price?" A female officer entered the garage to join Julia and Ellis. The woman was about Julia's height but probably had a good ten pounds of muscle on her.

"Yes, I am," Julia said as she got out of her car.

"Would you like to go inside before we start this?" the officer asked.

Julia nodded. She needed to sit. Take off her shoes.

"I'm Officer O'Hara," she said as she followed Julia into the house, all three of them entering through the garage door.

"Thank you for coming, Officer," Julia said, her shock and frustration beginning to wear off. In its place came gratitude that she had a multitude of people here to help her in this time of need.

Officer O'Hara nodded as she continued to follow Julia.

"We may want to avoid the front entryway for the time being," the officer said as Julia walked toward her office that was just off the front entryway. "There's quite a bit of broken glass. My colleagues are investigating, so we should go somewhere else until they get a better idea of what happened."

Julia nodded. That must've been how the man had gotten in. Julia had glass panels on the sides of her double front doors. Julia's breathing got shallow as she imagined a large, masked man coming into her home.

Julia realized if she allowed her emotions to get in the way, this evening would be filled with her hysterics rather than anything of value being discussed. That seemed like exactly what the man who had broken in would want, so Julia resolved to take a step back. Pretend she was playing a role instead of this being her life. Even though Julia typically delved into every emotion her character would feel, she would turn that part of her training off. She could play this part without feeling the frightening panic that was threatening to overwhelm her. She could do this.

She suddenly felt an arm going around her shoulders, and she immediately leaned into Ellis. His strength somehow rubbed off on her, and Julia no longer felt like she was going to fall over as she walked. Thanks to Ellis.

The three of them got to her living room, and Julia took a seat on the larger couch. Ellis sat right next to her, and Officer O'Hara took a spot on the loveseat on the other side of Julia.

"I've been told quite a bit by your security company, but it's important for me to get first-hand accounts," Officer O'Hara said.

Julia nodded. That made sense.

"Some of what I ask might seem repetitive, but please answer my questions," she continued.

Julia nodded again. She could do that, couldn't she?

Ellis's arm was once again around her shoulders, and Julia felt ready to take on this interview. She couldn't imagine how she would've felt if she were alone.

"Where were you this evening?" Officer O'Hara asked.

Julia told her Dax's address and the times she'd arrived and left.

"And did you not receive an alert from your security system?" Officer O'Hara asked.

Julia hadn't even thought of that. Thankfully, even in her fog, Julia had brought her purse out of the car with her and sat it on the couch next to her. She looked into her purse to find her phone and, sure enough, there was an alert from her security system. But she'd put her phone on silent for the wedding and hadn't noticed anything. She should've put her security system on another setting that would never allow it to be silenced, but Julia hadn't seen the need for that until this very moment.

"I did. But my phone was on silent," Julia explained.

Officer O'Hara nodded. "So how did you first hear about the break-in?"

Julia told the officer about the call and then answered a few more questions.

"Now we need to look over the security footage. Your security team sent over everything they had, but I think it would be best if we both look over the footage together," Officer O'Hara said.

Julia nodded. Although she didn't know if she was quite ready to see a large man invading her space, she knew she'd have to do it at some point, and she was glad she didn't have to be alone while watching a man breach the defenses of her home.

"The best place to watch the footage is in my office, and that's right next to the front door," Julia said.

Officer O'Hara nodded.

"We can also see the cameras from the kitchen, but it's harder to navigate the system. Probably the easiest way to pull up past footage is through my phone."

"Let's do that then," Officer O'Hara said kindly, and Julia was grateful her bedside manner was miles ahead of Duke's.

Julia opened her security app and saw that her security company already had a folder set up with all the footage of the break-in. She opened the folder and pressed play.

Julia cringed at the first shot: a man climbing what she had thought was an insurmountable wall.

"Does Julia have to watch this?" Ellis asked, gently taking the phone from her hands and pausing the video.

"We hoped she might see something that would help us identify the suspect," Officer O'Hara said. "We sometimes know the people who break into our home."

That made sense. Julia could do this. She was playing the role of a woman whose house had been broken into. She was tougher and stronger than Julia could ever be, and none of this was going to bother her.

"I'll watch," Julia said as she took the phone back from Ellis, shooting him a grateful smile as she did so. She appreciated him trying to shield her from the situation, but she could do this.

Julia watched as the man got to her front door, and without any hesitation, he punched the glass beside it. The man either knew Julia wasn't home or he didn't care. Her throat went dry. Nope, this wasn't her home. It was a character's home. She needed to focus.

"That glass isn't weak," Julia said, remembering how the man who'd installed it had said something about it being double paned.

"We think he must've had some sort of metal in his glove to help him punch through it," Officer O'Hara said, and Julia nodded, trying not to take it all in. "Might I suggest security glass when you replace it?"

Julia had been offered the nearly unbreakable glass when she'd first installed the windows, but it didn't appear quite as clear as the other glass and she hadn't wanted to mar her view. She figured her gate, her walls, and her security team were enough. Evidently not. Julia would need to look into replacing all the windows of her home soon.

"Yeah, that sounds like a good idea," Julia said as she watched the man push away the glass and slip through the window and into the home. The camera angle changed again, and this time her foyer camera caught the man pulling a rose attached to a note out of his jacket and leaving it on the ground. He then went back to the front door, unlocked and opened it, and fled back to the same spot of the wall. He was in and out of there in less than two minutes. Even with her security protocol, the cops had no chance of making it up there before the man was gone.

"Do you recognize anything about him?" Officer O'Hara asked.

Julia shook her head. The man was large like Duke had said. But he was covered from neck to toe in clothing, and a mask covered his face. There was nothing to see. Julia had tried to recognize the man's gait when he ran, but she had no luck.

"That's fine," the officer reassured as Julia closed her security app.

"We assume he parked down the street where there are no cameras," the officer said. "One of my colleagues is looking into how he approached your home right now."

This man knew her neighborhood. He knew that there wouldn't be cameras at all of her neighbors' homes. Julia fought the rising panic.

"How did he get over that wall?" Ellis asked.

"Apparently the intruder found a spot where there was a tree growing close enough to the wall to help him over. He used bushes just on the inside of the wall on the way back," Officer O'Hara said.

"A tree and bushes were allowed to grow tall enough to allow someone in?" Ellis asked, looking toward Julia. She could tell he was trying to keep his cool, but he was not happy about her security company's lack of foresight. Julia agreed. This was the exact thing they were supposed to prevent. But then again, they were trying to make up for it now.

"They're sending a technician up," Julia said, voicing her thoughts.

Ellis nodded, his face grim, but he didn't seem as upset as he had been.

"Do you use Avien?" he asked, and this time Julia nodded.

Ellis began to feverishly type on his phone as Julia's attention went back to Officer O'Hara. Julia was pretty sure Ellis used the same company for his security since Dax had been the one to suggest the company to Julia. She definitely didn't blame Dax, but the security company had truly messed up by allowing foliage to grow so close to her wall on both sides. She figured it was partially her fault also because, typically, officers worked with these systems. Whatever was lacking in the system would've been made up for by their highly skilled officers. But Julia hadn't wanted a stranger living with her, even if he was there for her security. So she'd opted out of that portion of Avien's services.

"I've never heard of Avien making this kind of error," Ellis muttered as he typed.

Julia hadn't either. But she guessed even the best had an off day. She just wished their off day hadn't resulted in this happening.

"Do you want to read the note the intruder left?" Officer O'Hara asked softly, pulling Julia out of her thoughts.

Julia really wanted to say *no*. She knew if she read whatever words had been left, they'd haunt her nightmares. But what if the words held a clue as to who this man was? And only Julia could decipher them? She had to be brave.

Julia nodded, her head feeling heavier than it should.

Officer O'Hara got up, coming back moments later with a dark red rose and a crisp white piece of paper attached with a black ribbon.

Julia felt her stomach drop, but she'd come this far.

The officer flipped the white card, and the few words read, "I'm dying to meet you."

Julia bit her lip as she scanned over the clue. The note was typed, so there would be no identifying this man's handwriting. The font of the note also gave away nothing, being that it was Times New Roman. So what did it mean? Julia scooted back from where Officer O'Hara stood holding the note in front of her, the little bit of bravery she'd had escaping her. There was nothing for her to figure out; she just wanted it gone.

Officer O'Hara turned and left the room with the rose and note, not saying a word to Julia as she did so. She seemed to understand that Julia wanted it out of her sight.

"Julia," Ellis said as he wrapped her in his arms. Julia leaned into his strength but knew she had to pull away soon. There was still work to do.

"We've been told your security team will be here in a couple of hours?" Officer O'Hara asked, and Julia nodded.

"Do you have anyone to stay with you until they show up?" she asked.

Before Julia could even think to answer, Ellis said, "I'll be here."

Julia looked over at the man beside her. Sometime in the last few minutes, he'd found her hand and held it. "You don't have to do that," Julia said, knowing she was asking a lot of the man.

"I know," Ellis said before looking back at the officer.

"Do you know anyone we can call to replace that glass?" Ellis asked Officer O'Hara.

"At this time on a Saturday? No. But a piece of plywood should work until you can call someone in on Monday," she said, and Ellis nodded.

"This is my card. Please call if you need or remember anything," Officer O'Hara said as she gave Julia her card.

Julia took the card and then looked up at the entrance to her living room when another officer joined them.

He shook his head slightly before leaving the room.

"Is everything alright?" Julia asked.

"Yes. It's fine. I think we're all set," Officer O'Hara said, standing.

"Can we clean up the glass?" Ellis asked.

"Yes, that should be fine," the officer replied. "Again, please call if you remember anything."

Julia nodded and then watched as Officer O'Hara left the room.

Julia listened as her front door opened and then closed. The police were gone. The house that had felt like a home just earlier that day now felt eerie.

"Come here," Ellis said as he gathered Julia in his arms.

This time Julia wasn't going to be brave, strong, or tough. The tears she'd been holding back came flowing.

As Julia cried, she felt Ellis start rubbing her back. The reassuring gesture caused Julia to really let go.

It could have been minutes or hours later when Julia

stopped crying. Time had seemed to stand still. When she pulled away from Ellis's shoulder, she saw black marks that her mascara had left behind.

"I'm sorry," Julia said, pointing to the marks. She knew if his shirt looked bad, her face had to be infinitely worse.

"Not even an issue," Ellis said as he stood, bringing Julia up with him. Even in her heels, Ellis towered over her causing her to realize that this man beside her had a good many inches on the intruder. And as Julia held on to him, she couldn't help but notice the muscles in his arms and back. As long as Ellis was around, Julia knew she'd be safe. That was a feeling she hadn't been sure she'd ever find again when she'd first been told about the break-in.

"How about you go change and get into something comfortable. I'll call my assistant and have him bring us some dinner," Ellis said.

"You don't have to do that," Julia said.

Ellis shook his head. "Stop saying that. I want to be here for you. I care too much not to," he said.

Julia was moved by his words, and she tried hard to make sure she didn't start crying again.

"Now scat," Ellis said as he shooed Julia away.

And she laughed. She actually laughed as she walked to her bedroom.

Julia took the back stairs since the front ones were in the foyer full of glass. She knew she'd have to take care of that at some point, but not tonight. Except she did have to find some plywood to cover the hole in her house.

Did she have plywood? Probably not. But she'd think about that later.

Julia got to her room, unable to close the door behind her. She didn't want any doors between herself and Ellis. She knew it was silly because he was a floor away, but she somehow felt safer with the door open.

First thing, Julia kicked off her torture shoes and put on her fuzziest slippers. She then took off her dress, replacing it with a pair of leggings and a huge sweatshirt. Finally, she looked in the mirror and nearly gasped at the trails of black streaks that nearly covered her face. Well, she'd heard it said that you should let a man see you at your worst. Check.

As Julia scrubbed her face, she swore she heard the sound of a vacuum. She thought about applying a bit of makeup after she'd washed it all off—she didn't want to see Ellis completely bare faced—but the sound of the continued vacuuming beckoned her. What was Ellis doing?

Julia was about to go down the back staircase again when she realized the sounds of the vacuum were coming from the foyer. Was Ellis cleaning up?

That got Julia moving. She jogged to the top of the stairs and then hurried down them just as Ellis turned off the vacuum. There wasn't a single shard of glass in sight.

Since the police had taken the rose and the note, the opening where the glass should've been was the only sign that anything had gone wrong that night.

A broom and dustpan full of glass told Julia that Ellis had not only vacuumed.

"Ellis," Julia breathed, unable to believe this man.

"Most people keep their cleaning supplies in the same place. I didn't have to snoop too much to find them," he said with a wink.

Julia felt herself falling hard for the man. How could she not?

"This should be good enough until the professional cleaners come in on Monday," Ellis added, and Julia's mouth dropped open.

"You hired cleaners?" she asked.

"I figured you'd want to wash out . . ." Ellis's voice trailed off.

All traces of the man who had broken in. Yes, Julia did. But for Ellis to think of that and then act on it?

"I scheduled them for the same time as the glass guy. Although, you'll probably want to get the glass guy to come back and do all of your windows with security glass. But I don't think he can do that on Monday," Ellis said.

"I only changed my clothes," Julia said, her eyes wide in amazement.

Ellis had cleaned her foyer, scheduled appointments, ordered dinner . . . and Julia had put on clothes?

Ellis chuckled. "I had some help," he said, holding up his phone. "My assistant on the island is taking care of dinner and getting some plywood. My team off the island is taking care of the rest."

"I forgot how nice it is to have people," Julia said.

Ellis grinned. "That it is."

"Maybe I need people again?" Julia asked, wondering if that would help. Did the fact that she chose to live on her own make her a target for men like the one who'd broken in? If she still had a team, would she be safer?

"Let's at least get you set with your security officer," Ellis said as he led her back into the living room.

Julia nodded. That would be nice. The thought of sleeping in her home alone . . .

Ellis sat Julia back down on her couch and then took the place beside her. Julia couldn't believe how safe and secure she felt considering what had happened that evening.

"I don't know what I would've done without you tonight," Julia said, trying to convey how much gratitude she felt with her words and her gaze. Did Ellis truly understand what he'd been for her?

"You would've been fine. You are a rock star, Julia," Ellis said with a confidence Julia didn't feel. But she was glad someone felt that way.

Ellis pulled her in to his side, and Julia melted into him. Butterflies tickled her stomach while at the same time, she felt secure and comfortable. How was that possible? Ellis was making her feel things she'd never even dreamed of experiencing, and at fifty-five, Julia had dreamed a whole lot.

The chime that alerted Julia to the fact that someone had arrived at her gate went off on her phone and the other camera stations in her home. Julia pulled out her phone to see a man in a shiny black pickup and looked over to Ellis.

"That's Les with dinner," he said, shooting Julia a grin that had her forgetting what a mess she was in.

Julia pressed the button on her phone to open her gate and watched Les as he drove in.

"Is that your pickup?" Julia asked, easily able to imagine Ellis behind the wheel of the monstrous truck.

"It's typically what I drive on the island, but I decided to dress it up with the Bugatti for Dax's wedding," Ellis said, referring to the car Julia had seen him driving. Julia thought about Ellis's multiple cars; she had a few of her own also. Their big homes, their need for security. They'd both achieved their dreams and the consequences, good or bad, that came with them.

"Did you ever think we'd get here?" Julia asked, thinking about her own childhood years and knowing Ellis's were pretty similar. They'd both come from working class families, and they were proud of it. But they sure did live different lives now.

"Honestly, yes," Ellis said slowly as he drew circles on Julia's exposed shoulder. She knew it had been smart to put on the baggiest sweatshirt she owned. "I had to. I had this fire inside that drove me, and if I didn't get to where I am, I think that fire might've just burned me right up," Ellis said.

Julia nodded because she could relate. But hers had been more like icy waters that she was running from. That was why she'd had to leave Travers. It had honestly felt like that icy water was going to swallow her whole if she didn't escape.

Fire and ice were a decent match, weren't they?

Julia's doorbell chimed, and Ellis yelled, "Come on in, Les."

"I figure he can hear us with that big hole in the wall," Ellis joked, and Julia chuckled, grateful they were no longer walking on eggshells. This made the night so much better.

Les came into the living room with bags upon bags of food.

"I hope you've got an army coming for all that food," Julia said as she watched Les drop the bags onto the coffee table.

"I just wasn't sure what you'd feel like," Ellis said, looking sheepish for the first time ever.

Julia laughed again. She liked sheepish Ellis. More than that, she liked seeing all these different sides of the man.

Ellis began digging through bags as Les left the room.

"Thank you for dinner," Julia called after Les.

"Not a problem," the man said in a drawl similar to Ellis's.

Julia raised an eyebrow that Ellis noticed. "We grew up together. He's held on to my tailcoats ever since."

"One, that's not the phrase. And two, you're lucky you have me, man," Les called back, obviously able to still hear their conversation.

Ellis let out a deep belly laugh that caused Julia to join him.

"He's right on both counts," Ellis said when his laughter subsided. "But we can't let him think I need him too much. Otherwise, he'll be asking for a raise."

"You're already scheduled to give me one on Monday considering you're making me work at eight pm on a Saturday," Les yelled.

Ellis shook his head. "Fine, but now you'll have to continue working weekends," he shot right back, and this time Les laughed.

"As if you ever gave me any time off before."

Ellis joined Les's laughter. It was easy to see that there was a deep friendship at the base of their working relationship.

"Now that the rude interruptions are over," Ellis said with a large grin, "what do you want for dinner? We've got dim sum, steak, a couple rolls of sushi—"

"Sushi?" Julia couldn't help but cut Ellis off before he said any more.

Ellis's grin somehow managed to go up a notch. "Salmon roll, veggie roll, or unagi?" he asked.

"Yes," Julia said, and Ellis chuckled as he handed a big, white box to her.

"Oh, it smells like heaven," Julia said as she opened the box and stuffed a piece of veggie roll into her mouth.

Ellis got a box for himself and then a pair of chopsticks.

"You use chopsticks?" Julia asked.

"I may look like a hick, but I can eat with the best of 'em," Ellis said.

Julia laughed. "They sure do make good looking hicks in Tuscaloosa," she said.

Ellis shot her a smirk. "Yes, ma'am, they do." Then he dug into his Pad Thai just as Julia heard hammering.

"Is he?" Julia pointed her own chopsticks in the direction of the front door.

"That's why I pay him the big bucks," Ellis yelled for Les, but he got no response. Not surprising since the hammering was so loud.

"Thank you again," Julia said.

"I need one thing from you," Ellis drawled in his sexy way.

Julia met his brown eyes.

"Stop thanking me," he said as he bopped Julia with the back of his chopsticks on her nose.

Julia giggled. "I guess I can try to do that," she promised.

Julia sank back on her couch, sushi in hand, feeling more safe and taken care of than she had in a long time. Thanks solely to the man she could no longer thank beside her.

CHAPTER THREE

"SEE YA, NORA," Mack called out as Piper and Nora made their way toward the gallery exit.

Ever since Kristie had introduced her mother, Piper, to Nora, the two had gone to coffee at least once a week. Piper's daughter, Kristie, was in the teen group that Nora and Mack regularly visited in the hospital. Kristie's terminal diagnosis had made her worried about her mom, thus the "friend set-up" with Nora. And boy was Piper grateful. She'd found that Nora was an incredible listening ear, and she hoped that Nora realized she'd find no more loyal of a friend than Piper.

"I'll miss you," Mack said, causing Nora to blush and Piper to grin. The man had it bad for her Piper's new friend. And yet Nora was unable to see it.

The door closed behind the pair, and they began to walk down Elliot Drive toward Grinds. It had the best coffee on the island and wasn't overrun with tourists at this time of day.

Piper was grateful for Mack's outrageous flirting. It helped her take her mind off of all that was going on in her life at the moment. She decided Mack was exactly the topic where her and Nora's conversation for the day needed to begin.

"I know you say he flirts like that with everyone," Piper said, to which Nora interjected, "He does."

"Not with me," Piper said as she turned to look at her friend. "I mean, I get that I'm a mom and old and everything, but I'd like to think I haven't lost all my feminine appeal."

Nora looked at Piper with both of her eyebrows raised. "Girl, you are all feminine appeal. Honestly, Mack is probably intimidated by you. I'm an easier target for his flirtations."

"Right, that's what's going on," Piper said with a shake of her head. But if Nora refused to see the truth, Piper wasn't sure she could make her.

"I'm glad you see things my way," Nora said in a teasing tone that told Piper she recognized the sarcasm but was going to ignore it. Piper was pretty sure that deep down Nora knew Mack had a huge crush on her, but if she was refusing to see the truth, she must not be ready for him. And Piper didn't want to push because she had a feeling that Nora and Mack were the real deal.

The two women ordered at the counter before finding a small table in the corner of the cafe. The cute little shop had pictures of Whisling through the years all over the walls and was full of tables that seated anywhere from two to eight people. Piper, being a transplant to Whisling, loved picking a new place to sit each time she came so that she could take in the pictures and learn the history of the beautiful island she'd made her home.

"Oh look. I think that was taken the year the high school was built." Piper pointed out a photo just behind Nora's head.

"Oh my goodness," Nora breathed as she turned to take in the picture. "This is so fun."

"Right?" Piper asked as Ginger, their cashier, brought their order over to them.

"Thank you," both women said as they dug into their blueberry scones. The coffee at the Grinds was incredible, but even incredible coffee couldn't compare to these scones. It was part of the reason why Nora took her lunchbreak at ten in the morning. These scones would be sold out by noon.

"Did Kristie decide to go back to school?" Nora asked softly as soon as Ginger walked away from their table.

Piper shook her head. That had been most of what their last conversation had been about. Piper's fifteen-year-old daughter, Kristie, had first been diagnosed with acute lymphocytic leukemia when she was seven. The diagnosis had been a blow to their little family. So much so that Piper's marriage hadn't survived. She knew there were many factors behind her marriage breaking, including the fact that it had already been brittle at the time of the diagnosis, but finding out their daughter was sick had blown the thing to smithereens.

But Carter had stuck around. Even though the last thing he'd wanted was to be stuck on an island like Whisling, even after Piper had told him it was over. He'd gotten a small apartment on Elliot Drive and went to every appointment, every chemotherapy session, every everything. Until Kristie finally went into remission nearly two years later. What a blessed day that had been.

But when they'd returned home from the doctor's that day, the three of them had known there was a possibility that it would all return. And it did. Five years later. Kristie was maybe the most angelic teenager there ever was, and Piper knew deep down she was just too good to be true.

When the doctor had said the cancer was back, it was Piper who had fallen apart. She'd tried so hard to keep it together, but it was just too unfair. Kristie had just gotten her life back and was even on the freshmen track team. That was how they had known. Kristie had started being too tired to go to practice. Not hungry, even after pushing herself to go on a three-mile run.

Carter had come back to the island immediately. He still lived in the cruddy apartment on Elliot Drive, just so that he could be close to Kristie. But it had only gotten worse. The doctors weren't sure if they caught it too late or if the cancer was more aggressive the second time around, but after another year of battle, the doctors told them there was no need for any more treatment. Kristie wouldn't win the fight this time.

Piper had never wanted anything more than to tell the doctor he could shove it. Kristie was a fighter; she could prove them all wrong. But then Piper had looked over at her little girl —so thin after months of chemo, a little hat on her head to cover her baldness, sallow bags under her eyes—and she shut her mouth. Her daughter had given this fight her all. And Piper's job was to let her know how proud she was of her. How incredible this little woman she'd raised had become. Fighting was done. It was now time to love hard. Oh so hard.

But Piper couldn't completely ignore the fact that the doctor had approximated that Kristie would have another six months to a year to live. Piper hated thinking about that date. Products should have expiration dates, not people.

With the time she'd been given, Kristie considered going back to school. She'd missed nearly all of high school so far and didn't know if she wanted that experience or more time at home. In the end, her body chose for her. Kristie just didn't have the energy to go to school each day.

"Is she . . .?" Piper could tell Nora was searching for the right word to fill in the sentence. Typically, if a high schooler wasn't able to go to school, one would ask if the teenager was okay with the decision. But could a person in Kristie's situation ever really be okay at all these days?

Piper had seen that Kristie could. She saw her daughter thriving, laughing, and even enjoying life, despite all the nasti-

ness she'd endured. But Piper could see why Nora was strug-
gling to get her thoughts out.

"She's doing well. And she at least convinced Brock to go
back without her," Piper replied.

Nora grinned, knowing how important it was for Brock to go
back to school. Both for his own family and for Kristie.

Piper loved that Nora knew these kids inside and out,
thanks to the time she spent volunteering at the hospital. Nora
knew that Brock had been given the green light to go back to
school after he'd gone into remission. They weren't sure he was
completely cancer free, but doctors were hopeful even as Brock
wasn't. The poor boy had fallen in love with Piper's Kristie and
couldn't imagine a world without the girl he loved. Piper
couldn't blame him.

"I bet he's hating it," Nora said.

Piper laughed. When she'd been told that Kristie had mere
months to live, she'd wondered if she'd ever feel the urge to
laugh again. To be happy again. But thanks to Kristie, she
laughed many times a day. Her sweet girl was all too perceptive,
and Piper knew if she gave in to the overwhelming urge to fall
into the depression that was never far off, Kristie would be the
first to feel it. Piper couldn't do that to her baby girl. So she
chose to laugh and live. She'd promised Kristie she would do so,
at least until . . . Piper refused to think about that day.

"He did at first. But then he realized his time at school gives
Kristie more moments to sleep. When he comes home, she isn't
nearly as tired as she would've been if she hadn't spent the last
fifteen hours resting. So it works out well for them."

"How does it work out for you?" Nora asked—all too perceptive, just like Kristie.

Piper shrugged. "They're young . . . and so in love. I honestly
wonder if they actually had the chance, if they'd be the ones to
break the high school romance stereotype. They're both so

beyond their years because of what they've gone through. Because of that, they treat each other with a kind of respect I wouldn't have even dreamed of as a kid. They are so good to one another," Piper said.

But instead of responding, Nora met her eyes. "You still didn't talk about you," she said.

Piper should've known Nora would pick up on that. And because of that perception, Piper blurted out something she wasn't planning on even telling Nora that day. "He wants to propose."

Nora gasped. Yeah, that was pretty much the same reaction Piper had had.

"They watched *A Walk to Remember*, so I should've known this was coming. Brock is such a romantic," Piper said.

Nora nodded. "But they're fifteen," she said, stating the obvious.

Piper nodded. "My thoughts exactly. It's all sweet and good in a movie. But in real life? Even just the logistics of life after they're married. They can't take care of themselves. What kind of marriage could they have? Then I remember I'm not a typical teen mom. I don't have to protect Kristie's future the way other moms do. We just have the here and now. Maybe in two years they won't be right for each other. But they don't have two years. We aren't even sure if we have tomorrow." Piper's voice broke, and Nora pulled her chair around the table to sit at her friend's side.

"So I gave him my blessing. He's actually going to do it today," Piper whispered.

Nora's wide eyes told Piper she had no idea how to react. Piper was fine with that. She wasn't sure how to respond either.

"I thought about saying no, but how could I do that? Kristie is going to miss out on so much of life. If she gets that moment to say *yes* and walk down the aisle . . . I just had to, you know?" Piper said.

Nora nodded, her eyes brimming with tears.

"But then this selfish side of me appears. Kristie is my little girl. Brock is already there so much of the time. If they get married, the little time I have with her all to myself will be over. And I can't give that away, can I? I honestly thought about saying *no* so many times. I really wanted to. I thought Kristie would understand. One day, when she was a mom, she would understand. That stupid, fleeting thought came. Before reality hit. Kristie will never be a mom. But I could allow her this opportunity to be a wife. Something she's always wanted. I know she loves Brock and he loves her. I can't judge if it's the deep, abiding love that you need to make a marriage work for a lifetime, but I don't have to. For now, it's so real for the two of them."

"So you said *yes*," Nora said, and Piper realized they both had tears streaming down their cheeks.

Piper nodded. "Carter wasn't happy with me. I don't think he would've ever been ready to let our Kristie get married. But I explained what I could, and Carter let it go. I think he understands that in this situation, we will never have the ideal. But we can work with good for now."

Nora bit her lip and just shook her head.

"It's a lot, right?" Piper asked.

"That's an understatement," Nora replied.

For some reason, Piper had to laugh. What Nora had said wasn't even funny, but Piper doubled over as she continued to laugh. Nora eyed her warily before the contagious laughter took over, and soon both women were laughing way too hard for such a mundane response to such a sad question.

"You never cease to amaze me, Piper," Nora said as their laughter finally died down.

Piper shook her head. She wasn't the amazing one. Kristie was.

"I have no idea what I'm doing. Half the time I feel like I'm walking blindly through life," Piper said.

"Well, *blind you* manages life much better than me with my eyes wide open," Nora said.

Piper teetered on the decision to smile or cry again, the same decision she struggled to make all day, every day since the diagnosis. This time, like most of the others, she settled on smiling.

"When is he popping the question?" Nora asked, and Piper looked down at her watch.

"Probably just about now. It's a teacher in-service day, and since they didn't have school, he wanted to take Kristie to the park where they first met. His mom had to drive them."

Piper knew that irony wouldn't be lost on anyone. This young man was proposing before he could even legally drive.

"He saved up for this really sweet ring and . . . he's so excited. Kristie will be thrilled." Piper smiled, thinking about her daughter's reaction. That was what mattered. Piper knew that in the months and years ahead, she would never regret allowing her daughter any extra moments of happiness.

"For what it's worth, I think you're doing the right thing," Nora said quietly.

Piper shot her friend a sad smile. "Honestly, right now that's worth everything. Thank you," she said, taking a sip of her now cold coffee.

"When is the next time Amber will come to visit?" Piper asked, realizing they'd spent their entire coffee date talking about her and Kristie.

"Hopefully in the next month or so," Nora said, but it was obvious to see her mind was still on Kristie. Then again, so was Piper's.

It was time to bring out the big guns.

"And things at the gallery are going well? I know that right now you're showcasing a certain hunk of a man," Piper said, causing Nora to burst out laughing.

"You did not just say that," Nora said through her laughter.

"Oh, I did. And I have no regrets," Piper replied.

Piper continued to pepper her friend with questions about her life, and before they knew it, it was time for Nora to get back to the gallery.

"Tell Mack I said *hi*," Piper said in a sing-song voice as the women got up from their table.

"You are too much," Nora said with a roll of her eyes as they walked out of the coffee shop and onto Elliot Drive.

Piper pulled her jacket tighter around her as the cool island wind hit them. The wind was one of Piper's favorite things about the island during the summer, but now that it was well into October, the wind had a bite to it that she wasn't a fan of.

"Same time same place next week?" Nora asked.

"Yeah. I'll let you know if my schedule changes, but so far the only shoots I have are in the afternoons for the next couple of weeks. Everyone loves afternoon and evening shoots in the fall."

Piper worked for a big photography studio on the island, doing most of their outdoor shoots. The job had been perfect, not only because Piper had had fairly flexible hours during the worst of Kristie's treatments, but the steady job had given her medical benefits, something they'd desperately needed in order to cover the bills and something freelancing photographers didn't get. The studio even allowed her to still take personal photography jobs when her schedule allowed. Honestly, she had lucked out in the employment department. Piper had to remember those blessings when it felt like the rest of her world was falling apart.

"Sounds good. Just let me know," Nora said as they got back to her gallery, where Piper had parked her car.

Piper gave her friend a hug. "Thank you for today. I didn't realize how much I needed it until it all came out."

"That's what I'm here for," Nora said, returned the hug.

"Don't have too much fun in there," Piper whispered as Nora opened the door. She had to get one last jab in before Nora went back to work. Maybe her friend wasn't ready for Mack, but Mack was more than ready for her. So if Piper could get Nora to a place where she would finally allow herself to be loved, Piper felt she could maybe give back a tiny bit of what Nora had given her.

Piper walked to her car, the few steps suddenly feeling like miles now that Nora was no longer with her. She needed to get home soon. She was guessing that she would be Brock and Kristie's first stop after Kristie said *yes*, and she needed to be prepared. Not just physically but mentally. She had to be in a place where she could rejoice with her daughter. Her fifteen-year-old daughter who would be getting married.

Piper was sure there would be people who would judge her for this. Tell her that Kristie and Brock were too young. And they were. They all knew they were. But these circumstances, cancer, changed everything.

As Piper started up her car, her phone rang. She connected it to her car's bluetooth before answering.

"Hey, Carter," Piper said, proud of where they were now.

Their divorce had been an ugly one. Especially because it was in the middle of all of Kristie's health issues. Piper had been so angry at Carter for even thinking about leaving the island. It was their home. It had been ever since Kristie was two. But he wanted to move them all closer to a Mayo clinic, or at least that was what he said. Piper knew deep down that the move wasn't just about Kristie. The care at Whisling Hospital would be superb, and when it wasn't enough, they were close enough to Seattle for other options. The move was because Carter was getting itchy. He had been for years.

Carter and Piper had married too young, another reason why Piper had been hesitant about Brock and Kristie. But their situations couldn't be more different. Brock and Kristie already had a kind of love that had weathered major storms, that had endured. Whereas Carter had fallen in love with the high school prom queen and Piper had adored the quarterback. It would've been a cute little love story had it not gone beyond those years. But it had. And they just weren't built on very much. So when the winds had come, and boy did they come, it had all blown down. So Piper had told Carter to leave. To move closer to a Mayo clinic or wherever he wanted to go. But she and Kristie weren't going anywhere.

Carter had stuck around on the island until remission, and Piper would forever love him for that, but he flew the coop when he could. And Piper was glad for that as well. Carter had needed that time away. He'd needed to grow up. And Piper was pretty sure that he had. Because of that time away, Carter could now call without resentment behind his every word. And Piper no longer felt like an anchor who was getting punished just for being who she was.

"Did they do it?" Carter asked.

Piper fought the urge to laugh. This man loved his baby girl, despite where their marriage had gone, and she knew today would be a hard day for him.

"I'm not sure. I'm headed home right now to wait for them," Piper said. She began to feel some compassion for Kristie's father. "Do you want to join me?" she asked.

That was all Carter needed. "I'll be there in ten."

Piper chuckled as the call dropped, and she drove the short distance back to the cute, little, blue and white, island-style home that she and Carter had once shared. Another point in Carter's favor: he'd never ever allowed Kristie or Piper to want for anything. Even as he'd traveled the world, he'd sent back more than the alimony and child support the courts had required. Even when things had been tight for him while he was building his career. He'd started as a travel reporter for a small magazine, his daily stipend nearly as much as his monthly salary. But he'd made a name for himself, and now Carter was at the helm of one of the biggest travel blogs and YouTube channels. They'd both started small, with Carter as the only traveler. But when he'd realized that the more places he went, the better the channel and blog did, he began to hire other travelers to film the places they went to and the foods they ate. Now he could run the whole thing from Whisling, even as he no longer traveled, because he wanted to be near Kristie.

Just as Piper got to her front door, Carter's car pulled up next to hers in the driveway. He jumped out, in a hurry the way he always was, and jogged to meet Piper before she could even get inside her home.

"You look good, Piper," Carter said as he gave his ex-wife a once-over and then headed into the house.

Piper felt her core warm at the compliment and decided she needed to be around more single men if all her ex-husband had to do was give her a sweet compliment and she was all melty.

Carter stood in front of the coat closet where he'd just hung his own jacket, ready to take Piper's. She handed it to him before heading into the kitchen to brew up a pot of coffee. Thanks to her latte at Grinds getting cold, she was now in dire need of a caffeine fix.

"Do you want some?" Piper asked as she began to get out the ingredients for her favorite at-home latte.

"Do you even need to ask?" Carter said as he joined her in the kitchen, his six-foot-two height and broad shoulders filling the small space. Because Piper's house was still the one she'd once shared with Carter, he felt completely at home whenever he came over. *Maybe too at home,* Piper mused as she watched him pull two mugs out from the right cabinet.

"So, we're happy about this, right?" Carter asked as he leaned against the butcher-block countertops that Piper had replaced herself three years before. She was still quite proud of the kitchen renovation she'd done. She'd repainted every cabinet a dark gray and then pulled out the old countertops and replaced them. All with just the help of YouTube. She'd like to one day replace her sink but figured she wasn't quite ready to take on plumbing.

"We're thrilled, Carter," Piper said as she finished making their lattes and handed one to her ex.

"Thrilled. Okay," Carter said as if he were pumping himself up before a football game. "This Brock is a good guy?"

"The best." Piper felt the unnecessary urge to protect this boy from Carter, even though Carter offered no threat. But Brock really was the sweetest and cutest boy. And the smile he brought to Kristie's face? It was enough for Piper to love him as well.

"I just . . . she deserves a lot, you know?" Carter said.

Piper nodded. She understood, even though Carter wasn't being very eloquent. But she knew her ex well. The man had no problem coming up with every word in the dictionary when it came to describing a sunset or an incredible bowl of curry, but throw some emotions into the mix and he fumbled his words every time.

"I know," Piper said, shooting Carter a soft smile. Even though Carter wasn't with her romantically, he'd been through this battle by her side. For better or worse, no one understood all of this better than Carter.

"With them being so young, I can't help but think about us. And you deserved so much more than you got," Carter said.

Piper almost took a step back at his honesty. That might've been Carter's truth, but Piper had seen a different side to it all.

"Neither of us was ready to love each other in the way we deserved," Piper admitted.

Carter looked up from where he'd been staring at the wooden flooring to meet Piper's eyes.

So much passed between them with that one gaze, but all of it was too raw to voice. They knew they'd hurt the other, and those pains ran deep. But they also knew they needed each other. Kristie, the tie that would always be between them, caused that need. Because when she passed on, they would both be the only ones left with the exact same hole. And that knowledge brought them together in a way nothing else could. Not even marriage.

"I guess you could be right. But those two are ready?" Carter asked.

"I'm not sure. But she deserves to watch a boy go down on one knee, be so in love with her that he trembles as she listens to him say the sweetest words a boy could. And she deserves to have the chance to say *yes*," Piper said.

Carter took a sip of his latte before nodding.

"She does. But I'm still sure this guy isn't worthy of her," Carter said.

Piper chuckled. She knew that in Carter's eyes, even after hundreds of years of scouring all the boys on the earth, there would be no one worthy of Kristie. And Piper loved him for that.

"And what kind of wedding are we talking?" Carter asked. "Wait, if they're getting married . . . they aren't living together, are they?"

Piper saw the way the situation was escalating and knew she needed to calm Carter before things got out of control.

She put a cold hand on Carter's warm arm, and he immediately went still.

"We'll cross that bridge when we get there," Piper said. She wasn't thrilled with the idea of the fifteen-year-olds living together either, but time got really skewed when cancer joined life.

"I'm never crossing that bridge," Carter promised.

Piper fought the urge to laugh. As much as this protectiveness was crazy, she also knew it was a big reason why she and Kristie had never lacked, even when Carter had practically hated Piper.

"Okay," Piper said calmly.

Carter huffed. "I know what you're doing," he said, looking down at her arm.

"Is it working?" Piper asked.

Carter shrugged, the closest Piper would get to an admission.

Suddenly the front door opened, and Piper's breath caught in her throat. She hadn't even heard Brock's mom's car pull into the driveway. They were here. They were home. And Carter was still too close to blowing up. But ready or not, they were about to play happy parents of the bride.

But then the door slammed shut and footsteps, one set, pounded, running for Kristie's room.

What the heck?

Carter and Piper exchanged a look before they both started toward the hall that led to the three bedrooms in the home.

Piper glanced down the hall toward where the door to her room stood wide open. The room she'd once shared with Carter. And now they were walking down this hall together. Nope. She needed to focus on Kristie. And the shut door right in front of them.

"Kristie," Piper said tentatively through the door.

A grunt sounded on the other side, and that was all the permission they needed. Carter opened the door, letting Piper through first.

Piper's heart broke as she caught sight of her daughter sprawled out on her stomach on her hot pink bed. When other little girls had asked for light pink and princess everything, Kristie had wanted hot pink and black. They'd decorated her room just after she'd gone into remission when she was nine. Piper had thought about redecorating since then, but then relapse had happened and survival had been most important. Until today. Should Piper offer to redecorate Kristie's room now? That was an idea she tucked away as she sat on the corner of the bed nearest to Kristie's head.

"Do you want to talk about it?" Piper asked.

Kristie shook her head.

"Do I need to kill that boy?" Carter asked, and Piper rolled her eyes.

"Dad?" Kristie looked up, obviously surprised to see her father standing in her room. She suspiciously eyed her dad and then her mom before a look of realization covered her face. "So you guys knew what Brock was planning?" Kristie's big, green eyes continued flitting from Piper to Carter.

Piper nodded. "Brock asked for our blessing," she said evenly, unsure of why Kristie was upset about this situation and, therefore, with her. She knew she needed to tread carefully.

"And you gave it to him?" Kristie asked, her eyes going wide.

Piper wasn't sure what she'd done wrong.

"She did," Carter said, pointing to Piper, and Piper glared in return. "Okay, we both did. But I did under duress," Carter replied.

Piper bit back a smile. This man was too much.

"What were you thinking, Mom? We're fifteen!" Kristie said as she sat up and leaned against the wall beside her bed, tucking a black pillow into her lap.

Piper drew in a deep breath, unsure of how to answer. Kristie was unhappy about Brock proposing to her? Piper had not seen this coming. And how was she supposed to answer Kristie's question? Piper guessed going with complete honesty was the only policy she could follow.

"I was thinking none of this is fair." Piper waved around the room, knowing she didn't have to explain what *this* was to anyone in that room. "And I thought . . . well, honestly I thought Brock proposing was what you'd want. You don't want that?" Piper asked, still feeling quite confused.

Kristie sighed as she dropped her head and cuddled the black pillow closer.

"I want to live a normal life, Mom. I know where Brock's idea came from, and *A Walk to Remember* was cute and all. But do you know why she got married when she did?" Kristie asked quietly.

Piper waited because she was guessing the question was one Kristie wanted to answer. "Because she was dying. Who wants that hanging over the most beautiful day of her life? I'd rather have this perfect dream in my mind of what the day would've been. And then when I get to Heaven, I'll ask God for it. I think he'd be happy to give it to me, right?" Kristie asked.

Piper fought back the tears. Her sweet, faith-filled girl. If only Piper could be half as good.

"I love Brock. With all that I know. But I'm fifteen. This is puppy love, isn't it? You can't get married on puppy love," Kristie said in a way that was beyond her years.

"We did," Carter pointed out unhelpfully in only the way Carter could, and Kristie's attention shot to her dad.

"Exactly! I can't do that too," she said as she pulled her pillow even closer to her. "But Brock doesn't get it. I think I made him cry, Mom." Kristie looked close to tears herself.

Piper's heart broke for her little girl who had already endured too much. She dropped to her daughter's bed, opening her arms wide, and Kristie eagerly crawled across the bed to be embraced. Piper knew Kristie's frustration was more at the situation than at any one of them, but Piper was more than happy to step up and take the blame if it made Kristie feel even the tiniest degree better.

"It's just . . . this cancer. It's taken almost everything, you know? Believe me, I get it. I understand reality even if I'm acting all happy and stuff. But I think I act the way I do *because* I understand the reality of the situation. Tomorrow this could all be gone, and if that's the case, do I want to spend today moping?" Kristie asked.

Piper shook her head, tears filling her own eyes.

Kristie was right. It was easy to deny that they were living on borrowed time, thanks to her upbeat personality. Piper sometimes worried that Kristie was living in a naive state, but if it brought her bliss during her last days, who cared? Piper bit down on her lip at the thought of the phrase *last days*. Those words should never be associated with any fifteen-year-old. Yet here they were.

"So it's better not to concentrate on the stuff the cancer has taken. My hair," Kristie said, reaching up to pull at the tufts that had grown back since her last chemo treatment. Losing her strawberry blonde hair had been rough on the sweet girl. But she'd endured. And then it had happened again. The second time had almost been worse, but then Kristie had decided to have a head shaving party. A few of her friends from school had joined, and even Piper had cut off all her hair. She wasn't sure she pulled off the pixie cut she now sported, but anything was worth supporting Kristie.

"I know I'll never get a driver's license, never go to prom," Kristie said, stumbling over the words. "But it's easy to forget when I'm just living life, you know? Because I hate being angry, sad, mad, and all the feelings that consume me when I let my thoughts start running wild. Being with Brock stops those thoughts. So I guess I don't really forget, but I've gotten good at moving my mind to another place. At pretending. And do you know what would make it really hard to pretend? Planning my wedding at fifteen." Kristie let out a sound that resembled a snort and a moan. Piper recognized this as Kristie trying to laugh through her pain. She'd done it many, many times before.

"I'll talk to Brock," Piper promised.

"I don't want him to . . ." Kristie began.

Piper held her daughter closer. "He won't feel like you blame him. I promise he'll come out of the conversation very pleased that you turned him down today," Piper said.

Kristie laughed. "Don't make promises you can't keep, Mama," Kristie said into Piper's chest.

Piper tried to laugh with Kristie but wondered how many more times she'd get to hold her baby girl like this. A handful? A dozen? However many times it would be, it wouldn't be enough. Yet Piper had no control over that. What she did have control over was how she lived the last days of her daughter's life, and they had both promised to live in the now. Piper had thought getting married was the epitome of that promise, but she could easily understand Kristie's point of view. She was sure Brock would too.

"That boy does love you. And if he knows this is what will make you happy, then he'll be fine. That I can really promise," Piper said.

"Really? Because after finding out you knew about this

proposal and did nothing to stop it, I feel like I can't trust you," Kristie said sassily, her eyebrow raised. Piper swatted her butt as Kristie laughed.

Out of the corner of Piper's eye, she caught the sad smile on Carter's face. It was a smile, but behind the smile was a look that said he knew he was going to have to say goodbye too soon. They all would. But Piper would wait until that moment to mourn. Because it was what her sweet Kristie wanted.

Sometimes as Piper lay in bed, waiting for sleep to come, she'd get glimpses of the all-encompassing pain that would greet her soon. The pain that would overwhelm her and bring her to her knees. She had no idea how she would endure, if she would endure. But at that point, it didn't feel like it would matter much. Her world, her Kristie, would be gone.

But when melancholy nipped at the edges of Piper's days, she continually pushed it away. Kristie was here now. That was all that mattered. It was all that could matter.

CHAPTER FOUR

"SO THE GIRLS are coming on the last ferry of the day?" Mack asked as he and Nora finished their typical cleaning routine after the gallery had closed for the evening. They'd had a red-letter sales day, so between that and her daughter coming for a visit, Nora was walking on air.

"No. They'll be here in a few minutes actually," Nora said as she looked down at her watch. She'd tried to talk her daughter, Amber, and Amber's adopted sister, Elise, into letting her pick them up at the ferry, but they wouldn't hear it. According to them, they were already stepping on her toes by staying in her tiny apartment with her. They weren't going to add bumming rides off Nora for their entire stay to the mix. The least they could do was rent a car.

Nora had given in because she was worried that the girls would take back their promise to stay with her if she pushed too hard about the car. They were all still finding their footing in this precarious world of after-adoption, and Nora wanted to give the girls the space they needed while spending as much time with Amber and Elise as she could.

Little did they know, the girls staying with Nora had been so important to her that she'd actually moved to a bigger apartment in her complex. Nothing huge, but when a one-bedroom unit had opened up near the studio apartment Nora had been renting, she'd jumped at the chance to upsize. Of course it cost a bit more, but it was totally worth giving her daughter and Elise a place to stay.

Besides, it wasn't like Nora couldn't afford it. She'd always lived with the mindset that she didn't have funds because she was intent on saving as much as possible. She tried to eat out as little as possible and spent little on her rent because she could. She liked to be cautious when it came to spending because she really enjoyed saving. Some women took pleasure in new designer handbags, luxury cars or even grand homes, but not Nora. She loved to see that little nest egg grow and grow. Though, to be honest, it wasn't very little anymore. She knew she should probably invest in something soon—maybe a home on the island—but for the moment, she was enjoying watching her account's contents grow and grow each time she made a deposit.

Nora shook her head free of the thoughts and saw Mack patiently waiting for her to come down from the clouds. She'd been spacing out a lot lately, and judging by the slight smirk on Mack's face, he enjoyed watching spacey Nora.

"Anyway," Nora said to the smirk, "they decided to catch an earlier flight instead of the one that would get them here at ten pm."

"I'm glad they did. I don't like the idea of those girls traveling too late in the evening on their own," Mack said protectively as he crossed his arms over his chest.

Nora raised her eyebrows in response. "Really? You do realize those girls are basically the same age you are," she said, her eyebrows raising higher as she spoke.

"You're joking, right?" Mack asked as he took a step closer to

Nora. The beautifully overwhelming scent of sandalwood and spice that was all Mack poured over Nora.

This was not good. Mack wasn't even a foot away from her, and he had that gleam in his eye. Nothing good could come from Mack looking at her like that. Or rather, maybe it was all too good. And that was what scared Nora. She knew if she allowed Mack in, it would change her—completely upend the little world she lived so safely in. And she wasn't sure she wanted that. No, she knew she wanted it. But she wasn't sure she was ready for it.

"I'm over a decade older than Amber," Mack said, his warm voice going deeper.

Oh, heaven help Nora.

"That's about a decade younger than me," Nora squeaked, and judging by the now full-on smirk on Mack's face, he'd caught it.

But Nora reminded herself of her words. That was a barrier between them. Nearly ten years. Who dated men ten years younger? Well, lots of women. But still, is that what Nora wanted? She glanced at Mack's dark blue eyes and chestnut hair. Yup, he was exactly what she wanted. Question was, was he what she needed?

Nora took a step back, her backside colliding with the reception desk of the gallery.

"Nora," Mack said softly, and it was nearly Nora's undoing. For a long time, she'd told herself her handsome coworker was a Casanova. A man not to be trusted who dated a new woman each night. But in the last couple of months, Nora had seen a new side to her coworker and friend. He had a past, sure, but who didn't? Nora sure as heck did. But in his present, Mack spent his time with teens who had cancer, worked hard at his career, and, according to him, no longer dated. At all. Like he hadn't gone on a single date in over six months. And Nora believed him.

Mack's deep blue gaze held Nora's, and she unwittingly took a step toward him. She knew what he was asking her; he'd been asking it for months. He wanted Nora to tear down the impenetrable walls she'd built, or at least let Mack scale them. He wanted her to let him in. Could Nora do it?

She looked down to see Mack holding out his hands. Physically, all it would take would be to join her hands with his. But it was the mental and emotional journey that seemed too far for one woman to traverse. Taking his hands meant telling Mack she was offering to open her heart. And her heart hadn't been opened to a man since she was nineteen. That terrible relationship had left a forever scar, one Nora had never cared to overcome.

But now she did. Now she wanted to allow a man like Mack into her life. But even though she was now on the downside of forty, this was a place where she felt she had no experience. It scared her to her core.

Nora lifted her hands just an inch from either side. Could she do this?

"Mama Nora!" Amber's sweet voice called from outside the gallery at the same time that loud knocking sounded on the front glass wall.

Nora jumped away, crashing into the desk behind her again, as she looked over to where Amber and Elise stood outside. Their wide grins told her they hadn't missed what had been happening between Mack and herself.

"Hey, girls," Nora said as she moved around Mack since it appeared the man wasn't going to budge. He hadn't jumped away the way Nora had. In fact, he hadn't moved at all.

"I can be patient, Nora," Mack promised as she walked past him, and her heart beat double time.

But now wasn't the time to think about Mack. Her girls were here. Although Elise wasn't her daughter biologically, or really, in any sense of the word, she'd found a special place in Nora's heart. The girl who had been such a wonderful sister to Nora's biological daughter was just as much Nora's family as Amber was.

Nora unlocked the front door and let the still grinning girls in, but she ignored their grins as she gave them both a hug.

"How was your flight?" Nora asked, and Amber shrugged.

"It was pretty turbulent, but the guy sitting next to Amber made up for the wild ride, didn't he, Sis?" Elise asked, nudging her now-blushing sister.

"He was a nice guy," Amber said, sounding a lot younger than her twenty-six years. From the little Nora had gleaned about Amber's dating life, it had been pretty much like her own in recent years. Nonexistent. According to Elise, her sister had been much too busy focusing on grades, sports, and then her career to care about the opposite sex. Unlike Elise, who had spent many of her free Friday nights on dates with some of Kansas City's finest.

"He was more than a nice guy, Amber. He was hot," Elise said before thumbing back at Mack. "Well, not as hot as that one. But close."

Elise pumped her eyebrows as Nora's cheeks went a deep red. One would think with Nora's deep complexion that it would be hard to see her blush, but thanks to her genes from her Caucasian mom, Nora's cheeks flamed with the best of them when she was embarrassed. And right now, they were on fire.

"I'm going to take that as my cue to go. But keep talking me up, Elise. I need all the help I can get," Mack said.

Nora couldn't even meet his eyes, she was so embarrassed. Did he think she'd talked to the girls about him? Would he assume she'd said things like that about him and that was why Elise was being so vocal about his good looks?

She needed to get a grip. Who cared if Mack thought she was interested. She was. And she was a grown woman. She could tell the man she was thinking about maybe possibly dating . . . okay, that was the issue. She didn't care that Mack knew what she felt, but she didn't want to get his hopes up. Nora from six months ago would've laughed at the idea that any woman could hurt Mack, but since those months, she'd learned Mack wasn't as aloof as he seemed when it came to his feelings. And he seemed to have some deep ones for Nora. She couldn't pretend they weren't there when she knew they were; it wouldn't be fair to Mack. But she still had no idea exactly where she stood. She liked the man. She admired him. She could possibly see her feelings growing into something more. That wasn't the problem. The problem were these dang walls she'd built, which had once been for protection but now felt like they were containing her. Keeping her from living life. How did she get rid of them? Especially when she was still scared of what could possibly happen if those walls came down.

All of her worries warred in her stomach as she felt Mack coming nearer. Her body knew that his was approaching. How?

Nora sucked in a breath as Mack stopped just beside her.

"Enjoy your evening, Nora. We'll pick up our conversation later," he said with a confidence Nora wished she could feel about anything in her dating life.

Nora's choices as a young adult had caused her so much heartache that she had maybe overcorrected in the ensuing years by exercising the highest degree of caution. That caution always had Nora feeling a bit insecure. Even though many applauded her art, she'd received a "best aunt award" from her niece, and she broke sales' records at the gallery left and right, she wasn't sure of any role she held in life. Especially those most important to her: mother and, maybe one day, girlfriend.

Giggling from Elise pulled Nora away from her thoughts, and she was reminded that her girls were just standing there staring at her.

"He is so cu-ute," Elise crooned toward Nora as soon as Mack locked the gallery door behind him.

Amber's phone dinged, thankfully taking Elise's attention from Nora.

"Is it him?" Elise asked, and Amber shrugged without looking at her phone.

"Are you really not going to check?" Elise asked, trying to peer into Amber's purse where her phone was.

"I will. Just not yet," Amber said, sounding very much like Nora.

Maybe some things really are more nature than nurture, Nora thought with a smile. But it was now time to save her daughter.

"Are you girls hungry?" Nora asked, and Elise nodded emphatically as Amber grinned at Nora.

"We could go fancy or we could get some burgers at Ava's." Nora offered.

"Burgers," the girls announced in unison, and Nora liked the idea as well.

"Do you two want to drop your car and luggage at my place? Then we can head to the diner from there," Nora suggested.

The two exchanged a quick look before Amber answered for both of them as Elise rubbed her stomach, "Let's just get dinner."

Nora smiled in understanding. Traveling somehow did make one quite hungry. She never understood it because traveling typically consisted of a whole lot of sitting, but she was always famished after a long day of travel. Maybe it was because she didn't usually like the food served on planes? Who knew.

Nora led the way out of the gallery and then locked the door behind them as the girls walked out into the cool, dark Whisling evening air.

Amber, Elise, and Nora tugged their coats closer to them in unison as they walked against the wind that was quite strong this close to shore.

"This place is absolutely gorgeous, but I could do without the winds," Elise said loudly over the sound of rushing air.

"They aren't always this bad, but yeah, nights like this can be quite chilly." Nora had to practically yell to be heard over the sound of the wind.

The girls rushed into their cute, little, red rental car as Nora pointed three parking spaces down to her sensible, gray sedan so that they'd be reminded about which car to follow.

Nora pulled out onto Elliot Drive and saw that the red rental was right behind her before taking the few blocks to where Ava's Diner was located. Fortunately, both cars were able to get parking spaces right in front of the diner.

Nora took in the large windows that were decorated with orange, brown, and yellow leaves for fall. She loved that Ava's glass was always decorated for the season.

"This is so homey," Elise declared as the three women rushed into the diner and then shook off the chill once inside.

"And the decor isn't even the best part about the place," Nora promised as they were greeted by Ava herself.

"Just the three of you tonight?" Ava asked.

Nora nodded. She'd thought about inviting Deb, Luke, and Amber's cousins along for dinner but decided she wanted this night with just her girls. Tomorrow she'd happily include their extended family.

"I'll be along to take your order in a minute. Chuck called in sick, so we're a little understaffed tonight, but I promise the food will be as great as always," Ava said with a big grin before rushing along to her next task.

Nora looked around at the other booths in the diner, and about half of them were full. Pretty busy for a Tuesday evening outside of tourist season, so she could see why Ava felt a little slammed.

She quickly perused the menu and decided on a BBQ bacon cheeseburger and onion rings. That sounded like exactly what she needed on this cold evening. She set her menu down at about the same time Elise did.

"I was hoping they would have a guacamole burger. Ava's Diner just made my night," she said with a wide smile. This girl seemed to love food as much as Nora did.

"It *is* the West Coast, and we *do* love our avocados," Nora said.

Elise laughed. "Right? I can't say I blame you all," she responded. "But the real question is, sweet potato fries or tater tots?"

Nora pretended to be deep in thought, her eyes squinting and her mouth dipped into a frown much too dramatic for the situation, making Elise laugh again.

"I get it. It's not a world-altering decision. But if I pick the wrong one, we'll have to be back here tomorrow because I'll surely have food regret," Elise said matter-of-factly.

"I can think of worse fates," Nora countered with a laugh.

Elise nodded. "True. I'm gonna go tots, and we'll just see how it goes," she said, clutching the menu to her chest as if she were taking her life into her own hands. This woman was too much, and Nora loved it.

"How is planning for the Romano wedding going?" Nora asked Elise since Amber was still looking through the six pages of menu.

"Fine. The bride is great, but her mother? Let's just say I've never met a bridezilla worse than this mother-of-the-bride," Elise said.

Nora cringed. She'd heard enough stories about the girls' wedding planning to know they'd come across quite a few difficult brides.

"But it will all be worth it when Rochelle finally hands the reins of KC Weddings over to us," Elise breathed out wistfully.

Her girls had been scrimping and saving to be ready for the day their boss decided to retire. Rochelle had seen how hard Amber and Elise worked and how good they were at what they did. She'd promised them that when retirement came, she'd sell KC Weddings to them.

"Is there a timeline for that blessed event?" Nora asked.

Elise glanced over at Amber who looked at her sister over her menu.

"I wanted to tell her in person," Amber said defensively as Elise shook her head. Then Amber looked at Nora. "We should be getting a call from Rochelle tonight," she squeaked, and Nora yelped loud enough that at least half the patrons in the diner looked their way.

"Seriously?" Nora asked, not caring about the attention they had received.

Amber nodded. "Rochelle's husband had a stroke," she said.

"Oh dear," Nora breathed, but Amber dropped her menu and put up her hands, the universal sign that everything was okay.

"It didn't have any lasting effects, thankfully," Amber said, and Nora nodded. Thank goodness. "But it did get Rochelle to thinking. She was considering retiring in the next five years, but the stroke bumped up her timeline. She thinks she might want to sell now," Amber said quickly, and Nora couldn't help her grin. This was huge for these girls. Life changing.

"She's having a big discussion with her whole family tonight, and she's going to call us as soon as she's announced to her kids that she's retiring. We'll have to work out some sort of a deal since we don't have quite enough saved." Elise said the last words with a tinge of worry, but she shook it off quickly. "I'm sure we'll work it out. We can always sell our condo. Places around us have been going for much more than we paid, even though we've only been there for a little over a year. We'll work it out."

"I'm sure you will. And if you guys wouldn't mind, we could always talk about me investing. I've been looking for a sound place to put my money," Nora said, remembering her thoughts from earlier that evening.

"You don't have to do that," Amber said with a swift shake of her head, seeming hesitant to allow Nora to take the leap with them. "I don't know if a business like ours is a sound investment."

Even though Nora had said the words on a whim, the more she thought about investing in the girls, the more she liked the idea. They were hard workers. She knew whatever Rochelle had already built, the girls would continue to grow. She wanted to be part of that. She hoped to prove it with these next few words.

"I wouldn't be investing in just the business. I'd be investing in you girls. And I know that *is* a sound investment," Nora said.

Elise grinned. "When Mama Nora is right, Mama Nora is right," she said, and Amber chuckled.

Nora had thought her daughter was a bit more quiet than usual that evening. Hearing what was on the line, now it made sense. Amber did tend to shut down when she was nervous.

"Alright, what can I get for you?" Ava asked, causing all three women to look up at her as she gathered the menus on the table.

"I'll get the BBQ burger," Nora ordered.

"With fries and a shake?" Ava asked.

Nora looked out at the chilly evening and shook her head. "Make that onion rings and a slice of pie. What kind do you have tonight?"

"Apple, cherry, boysenberry, and kiwi lime," Ava rattled off.

Nora's mouth began watering as she considered her options. "I have to go with kiwi lime," she stated, wondering if it would be bad to order all four pie options.

"Kiwi lime?" Amber asked.

"It's Ava's take on key lime. So good," Nora said.

Elise's eyes lit up. "I want one of those too," she ordered, along with her burger and tots.

"I think I'll go with the BBQ burger as well. But let's do sweet potato fries." Amber was already nodding before Elise could ask her to share some with her. "And I know I want a fruit pie, but which one?"

Ava grinned. "They're all good, if I do say so myself. We can all our fruits in house, but the apples are still fresh this time of year."

"I'll go with apple then," Amber said.

"Good choice. Your meals will be out in a jiff," Ava promised as she walked away, and the women fell back into their earlier conversation.

"We'll talk about you investing when the time comes, but first we have to see what Rochelle says," Amber said.

Nora nodded. She knew her daughter wasn't one to count her chickens before they hatched.

"Rochelle is going to say exactly what Rochelle has been saying for the last two years. We are the best people for her company's future, and she'll work with us so that we can take KC Weddings into the greatest years it's ever seen," Elise said confidently as she sat up in her booth.

"Yeah, of course she is," Amber said, but the doubt in her eyes was easy to see.

Elise either didn't see it or ignored it because she moved on.

"Now that we've got food on the way, are you going to check that text or not?" she asked Amber.

Nora bit back a chuckle. That Elise could be like a dog with a bone.

Amber rolled her eyes, and as much as Nora loved that Elise had a strong personality, she was glad her mild-mannered daughter didn't allow herself to be pushed around.

Elise began to lean over Amber to gain access to her purse as the latter pushed her away when Elise's phone began to ring.

"Saved by the bell," she muttered to Amber as she dug into her own purse and pulled out her phone.

"It's Rochelle," Elise gasped, and Amber's eyes went wide. Even Nora's stomach dropped. She knew how much this call meant to her girls.

"Hello." Elise wasted no time in taking the call, a huge grin on her face. Fortunately, the diner was devoid of any loud, rambunctious groups that evening.

Elise nodded once about a minute later but hadn't said another word after *hello*. Apparently Rochelle had a lot to say. That could be a good sign.

But then Nora watched as Elise's grin began to fall, slowly but surely.

Amber leaned closer to her sister, probably to offer comfort as well as try to listen in on the call.

"I get it. They're family," Elise said robotically, and Amber began shaking her head.

"How were you supposed to know, Rochelle?" Elise continued. "They showed no interest in KC Weddings before."

Elise was quiet for another moment.

"Yeah, I'm sure the stroke has you all thinking about the

future in different terms. Your kids want to carry on your legacy. That's sweet," Elise said. Her voice cracking over the word *sweet* was the only thing that gave away how she was truly feeling.

"We're disappointed," Elise said, and Amber nodded, "But we understand."

Amber nodded again but more slowly this time.

Nora wanted to grab the phone from Elise and tell this Rochelle woman what her unserved promises were doing to her girls. But she knew it would help nothing. It definitely wouldn't help her girls feel any better.

"Yeah. I think we will. We're on Whisling with Mama Nora, so we'll probably stay through the weekend?" Elise said as a question that was directed toward Nora.

Nora nodded emphatically. Of course her girls could stay with her as long as they wanted.

"We'll see you Monday." The false cheeriness had bled out of Elise's voice, and all that was left was defeat.

"I'm so sorry," Nora said as soon as Elise got off the phone. Amber wrapped her arms around her sister, and Elise dropped her head onto Amber's shoulder.

"I was so sure," Elise said.

Amber nodded. "We both wanted it so badly," she replied.

"Yeah, but you knew this kind of thing could happen. I was so blissfully blind," Elise said into her sister's shoulder, Elise's blonde hair mixing with Amber's black.

"There was no reason for me to feel it could fall apart except for my pessimistic nature. Of course you were sure it wouldn't fall through. You're an optimist," Amber said.

Elise laughed dryly. "Look where that got us. To the same place," she groaned.

"Is there no chance?" Nora asked, not wanting to pry but wanting to be sure of things before she commiserated. Maybe this could be salvaged?

Elise nodded. "Her daughters want to take over. They've been at home with their kids but are both getting antsy to get out into the workforce again. They felt like this was a sign. Rochelle didn't have the heart to tell them she hadn't even considered passing down her legacy to her own kids. She feels terrible."

Nora shook her head. Honestly, Rochelle should. She shouldn't have promised anything to the girls without being completely sure. It wasn't fair.

A young woman came to their booth laden with plates of burgers and pies.

"Just in time," Elise said as she looked at the overabundance of food.

"We'll eat our weight in comfort food and then go to sleep. Morning is always brighter, right, Mom?" Amber asked, and Nora felt her heart flip. Amber had called her *Mom*. It was the very first time. Sure, Nora loved the moniker "Mama Nora," but something about the simple word *Mom* warmed her to her very core.

"Definitely," Nora promised. And that was a promise she would keep.

CHAPTER FIVE

ALEXIS STOOD in the middle of her typically tidy living room, taking in the smorgasbord of flowers that had overrun the place.

Margie had decided that she and her bridesmaids, Alexis and Lou, would make their own bouquets from craft store flowers. Alexis was a bit intimidated by the task—she didn't have a crafty bone in her body—but she was ready to take it on. For her mother's sake.

Alexis knew Margie was still hurting because Marsha, Lou's sister, wouldn't be involved in this day or any other wedding event. Margie had hoped against hope that this marriage with Bill would be the union of two families, but Marsha wasn't going to allow that to happen.

"Do you think I have everything we'll need?" Margie asked as she began to pick up items like floral tape and wire cutters.

"That and more," Alexis said before quickly biting down on her lip, regretting her word choice.

"Do you think I got too much?" Margie asked the question Alexis knew was going to come after what she'd said. What she should've been too sensitive to bring up.

Ever since Marsha had accused Margie of being a gold digger after Bill's money, Margie had gone above and beyond to be frugal. Way more than she had to be, even on her income alone. She had refused to allow Bill to pay for dinners out, insisting on paying half. Bill hadn't been pleased about that turn of events, but he could see it meant a lot to her, so he'd given in. She had also insisted on signing a prenuptial agreement and was now planning the most simplistic wedding of all time. It couldn't have gotten that expensive, considering they were keeping the wedding guest list to the closest family and friends. And not even all of them would be coming. Bill had invited Marsha's ex-husband, Jared, and their kids, but Jared had informed Bill that he couldn't bring the kids without Marsha's blessing. Which Alexis understood. But she hated that the family was being torn apart, forced to choose sides.

So the tiny wedding was now going to be an ultra-frugal one as well. Thus the craft store flowers instead of fresh ones. Margie had also gone to the clearance section of each department store in their mall to choose her wedding dress, and she had instructed Bill to wear a suit he already owned instead of buying or renting a tux for the big day.

"You know that's not what I meant," Alexis said, trying to bite back the sigh she felt. How was Marsha dictating this day when she was refusing to even go to the wedding?

"I mean, I'll be sure to return anything we don't use and—" Margie began, but Alexis put what she hoped was a calming hand on her mom's forearm.

"Mom, it's great. Didn't you say you got all the flowers on sale anyway? I'm sure you couldn't have spent any less," Alexis tried to reassure all while hating Marsha.

Not only had Marsha complicated Margie and Bill's relationship, she was doing the same with Alexis's fledging relationship. Sure, Alexis was dating Marsha's ex. But Marsha had been especially vindictive and unfeeling. It made the relationship much more complicated, but Alexis had fallen. And she couldn't choose the baggage of the man she was starting to love.

Wait, did she love Jared? It was too soon, wasn't it? Instead of dwelling on that scary thought, Alexis turned her mind to the name she'd used when thinking about her boyfriend. She was still getting used to calling Jared by that name. She'd known him as Ethan back in high school when she'd had a huge crush on the guy. But after he'd married Marsha, he'd started going by his middle name. Since the entire island and those who Alexis loved called Ethan by Jared, Alexis realized she needed to hop on that train. Even though, deep down, she would always think of Jared as Ethan. The sweet boy of her high school dreams turned into the charming leading man in her life.

"Maybe I don't need these." Margie began to gather up a bunch of beautiful orchids. Alexis knew for a fact they were Margie's favorite flower. "They were the most expensive, and I probably shouldn't have splurged."

Alexis had had enough.

"Mother," she said sternly as she took hold of both of her mother's shoulders, causing Margie to drop the orchids. "This is your wedding day. The only one you've ever had. The only one you'll ever have. Please don't let Marsha destroy it. She already isn't coming. She's done enough. Now it's time to think about you and Bill. You know it's killing him that you're insisting on keeping your money separate. And that you won't allow him to shower you with the wedding of your dreams. But this penny pinching when we know you can afford those orchids on your personal salary? I can't allow for it, Mom."

Alexis loosened her grip on her mother's shoulders, pulling Margie into a hug. It looked like she needed it.

Margie nodded as Alexis held her, as if she was taking in what Alexis had said.

"I'll keep the orchids," Margie finally said. Then she pulled away from Alexis. "And maybe I'll stop insisting we go Dutch when we go on our dates," Margie conceded.

Alexis smiled. "I'm sure that will make Bill happy," she said.

Margie nodded. "I get what you're saying. I can feel Bill cringe anytime I refuse to accept anything from him—I know it's driving a wedge between us—but I can't help it. Marsha was right—" Margie began, but Alexis intervened.

"No, she wasn't," Alexis said, even though she wasn't quite sure what Margie was saying Marsha was right about. But when it came to any of this, Marsha was not right.

"Hear me out," Margie said as she plopped onto the one seat of their couch that wasn't overrun with flowers.

Alexis cleared herself a spot on the floor so that she could sit as well and gave her full attention to her mom.

"When I started dating Bill, part of me breathed a sigh of relief. I knew that Bill was well off, and as long as I was with him, I wouldn't ever have to worry about my income not being enough," Margie said.

"Mom—" Alexis started, but Margie raised a hand, so Alexis went silent.

"When Marsha said those things about me being a gold digger, at first the claims seemed incredible. I would never use Bill for his money. But then I started to realize that even if I wasn't dating Bill just for his money, it was an attractive quality about him. Marsha was right."

Alexis fought the urge to roll her eyes. Her mother had truly been convinced by her soon-to-be, evil stepdaughter that she, Margie, was a gold digger. The same Marsha who'd left her husband, Jared, because she wanted to stay with her rich lover. The same Marsha who put someone's monetary worth above all else.

But her mother was hurting, and that was the only reason Alexis was taking any of this seriously.

"Mom, a man's ability to provide for you *is* an attractive quality. That's biology, not some deep-seated issue with you," Alexis said.

But Margie shook her head, still unconvinced.

So Alexis thought of a different tactic. "Mom, how often do you plan on cooking for Bill?"

Alexis knew for a fact that her future stepdad was a terrible cook. So bad that Lou had begun sending frozen meals over to him every few weeks just so that he would stay out of his kitchen.

"Every night we're home," Margie said.

"I know that your talents in the kitchen are part of what attracted Bill to you. So do you feel like Bill is using you?"

Margie tilted her head and raised her eyebrows at Alexis, telling Alexis she wasn't amused.

"That's not the same thing," Margie said.

"Isn't it? You are bringing something, in this instance a skill, to your marriage. The same way Bill is doing with his money. You will be uniting every part of you. There's nothing wrong with that," Alexis said.

This time Margie pursed her lips as if she was finally taking it all in.

"And of course you'd break up with Bill if he lost his money." Alexis went in with her final point, and judging by the shocked expression on her mom's face, it had hit its mark.

"Of course not," Margie replied indignantly.

Alexis laughed. "Of course not, Mom. I know that; you know that. Marsha doesn't. But really, Mom, why do you care what Marsha thinks? Bill doesn't."

Margie nodded, leveling Alexis with a look she knew well. It was the one that Margie gave when she was finally yielding.

"So I win?" Alexis asked cheekily.

Margie chuckled. "You win. I'll talk to Bill and tell him my insecurities. Then I'll let him pay for the stuff he wants to."

"And ask him for help if you need it?" Alexis asked.

"Now that might be taking it too far," Margie responded quickly.

"Mo-om," Alexis said.

Margie gave her a tiny smile. "I'll try."

"That's all I can ask," Alexis said as their doorbell rang, alerting them that Lou and her tribe must've arrived.

Alexis opened the door, surprised to just see Lou and her daughter, Hazel. Alexis peeked around the two, looking for Lou's other three kids, but they weren't there.

"Harvey came through for once," Lou muttered under her breath in an attempt to keep Hazel from hearing what she'd said.

"Harvey isn't a good-for-nothing anymore," Hazel said, sounding like she was parroting someone else's words, and both Alexis and Lou cringed.

"No he isn't. And let's not say that again," Lou said to her five-year-old who was apparently going on thirty-five.

Alexis hadn't spent too much time with Lou's kids since good-for-nothing Harvey had actually been taking them the two days a week their court documents specified for the past few months now. Way better than in the past. And Lou was actually starting to not hate her ex.

But because the kids were gone most weekends, and that was when Alexis and Lou typically hung out as well as when they both worked at the gym Bill owned, Alexis didn't know Lou's kids as well as she would've liked. Now that she was going to be their step-aunt, it was about time she got to know them. She was excited to start with cute, tow-headed Hazel. Alexis could totally picture Lou looking the exact same at that age.

"Hello, Hazel," Margie said as she came around the wall that partitioned the kitchen from the entry way. "Would you like a snack?" she offered, already winning awards as best Gammy ever.

Gammy was the name she'd decided to take as a grandmother. Alexis hadn't known choosing your "grandmother name" was even a thing. She'd naively assumed that when you became a grandma, you went by the name the kids called you. But oh no no. There was a whole process. The grandmother chose a name she liked, the parents had to approve, and then you'd cross your fingers the grandkids could actually say the name. Bonus points if they could say the name as their first word. Since all of Margie's new grandkids were already of speaking age, they could say the name with ease. The time for bonus points had expired.

"Yes please, Gammy," Hazel said as she took her Gammy's hand and skipped into the kitchen, her little pigtails flying to and fro. Why couldn't pigtails look that cute on a grown adult?

Unlike Alexis, Margie had spent quite a bit of time with her future grandkids. She'd cheered them on at baseball games, soccer games, and even a piano recital. Alexis hadn't been invited to most of those activities because her own dating life complicated things. She and Jared had decided it wasn't quite time for Alexis to meet his kids. Who were also Marsha's kids and Lou's kids' cousins. Therefore, they were usually at the aforementioned games, unless their mother forbade it because she'd known Margie was going to be there. Fortunately, that didn't happen too often. Marsha wasn't too in tune to who her kids were interacting with because she was in the thick of trying to win back her rich lover, if island gossip could be believed. But, unlike Marsha, Jared was always an involved parent, putting his kids' well-being above his own. And even though he wanted to introduce the kids to Alexis, it seemed just a little too soon. His kids were still finding their footing post-divorce.

"So we've got some flowers here." Lou interrupted Alexis's thoughts as she perused the living room.

Alexis laughed. That was the understatement of the year.

"You ready to make your bridesmaid bouquet?" Alexis asked.

Lou shrugged. "Ready as I'll ever be," she said as she sat down on the spot of the floor Alexis had vacated to answer the door. "These are pretty," she said as she began to pick up various flowers.

Alexis nodded. All of the flowers were pretty. It was hard to tell that some were even fake. Artificial flowers had come a long way since Alexis was in high school and had helped her class create a fake flower float for homecoming.

Lou continued to pick up this flower and that, and by the time Alexis looked over again, she'd put together a bunch that was the epitome of a perfect bridesmaid bouquet. Of course Lou would be good at this as well. The woman had no short-comings.

"Gammy gave me the biggest piece of chocolate cake left," Hazel bragged cutely as she came walking in from the kitchen with a ginormous piece of cake.

"A piece of cake you had better share with Mommy," Lou said as she shot Margie a look that daughters around the world sent to their mothers when said mothers were overindulging the grandchildren.

Margie just grinned. "This was all that was left," she said in defense.

"You could've told her it was six pieces," Lou reprimanded, but Margie just kept on grinning.

As terrible as Margie's relationship was with Marsha, it was the absolute opposite with Lou. Although Lou had had a bit of a hard time when she'd learned her father was marrying Margie just a year after her mother had passed, she was able to quickly admit this new marriage was what was best for not only her dad but for their whole family. It'd taken about two weeks before Lou had welcomed Margie into the family with no reserve and open arms.

"I could have," Margie said with an unapologetic shrug, and Lou just sighed.

"Grandmas," Lou muttered, causing Alexis and Margie to laugh. Hazel joined belatedly, loving that she was in on some joke she didn't understand.

"Grandmas," Hazel repeated, and this time Lou joined in the laughter.

Hazel dug into her cake, and Lou stopped laughing in order to man the chocolate cake consumption.

"What do you think of Lou's bouquet?" Alexis asked Margie as the other two concentrated on cake.

"Oh, it's perfect, Lou," Margie gushed as she inspected the bouquet Lou had put together in just a few moments. Alexis would be lucky if she got hers done before the wedding.

"Thanks, Margie," Lou said as she looked down at the flowers she'd gathered and then quickly back at the cake. "I didn't have bouquets at my wedding, so I never would've thought I'd like them so much. But it's kind of fun, right? Holding our very own flower arrangements," she said with a grin before swiping the fork from Hazel. She'd taken six bites in a row, and Lou knew the whole gigantic piece would be gone if she didn't intervene now.

"You didn't have a bouquet?" Alexis asked.

Lou shook her head. "We got married when we were eighteen, and Dad was so upset about the whole thing that he hardly gave Mom a budget to plan the day. We had to cut quite a few corners, but now I'm glad. If I'd had a picturesque wedding day only to discover the marriage itself was crap, what a sore disappointment that would've been. With a subpar wedding day, I was kind of prepared for what came next," Lou joked.

But Alexis knew her friend well enough to know her joking often covered her pain. Lou hated that her marriage had failed. She hated even more that she'd brought kids into the mix.

"That cake was delicious," Hazel said, and Lou gasped. The kid had eaten the whole thing while Lou had been busy talking. Alexis didn't know whether to applaud her or laugh.

She glanced at Lou's narrowed eyes and decided on neither.

"I thought we were sharing," Lou said.

Hazel's big, blue eyes went round. "We did share. I gave you four bites."

How was it that kids could remember those kinds of details so vividly?

"That wasn't enough. That was a huge piece of cake."

"I'm sorry, Mama," Hazel said with such pure intent, Alexis doubted Lou could stay angry.

"That's alright, Bug," Lou said as she wiped Hazel's mouth with a baby wipe she'd seemingly produced out of nowhere. "But we're here to work," she said, and Hazel nodded as she began to examine the flowers. "I brought this one because she promised she'd be a big helper."

Hazel nodded, her big eyes seeming to go even wider. "I'm a really good helper," Hazel promised Margie, and the latter couldn't help her gigantic grin. "And Mama said coming today can show Gammy how glad I am that she's joining our family. Now that Nana is in Heaven, Papa Bill needs help here on earth. And you seem like the best big helper too, Gammy," Hazel said.

Now Margie's grin was accompanied by wet eyes. Alexis could only imagine how much those words meant after the hard time Marsha had been giving her.

"So you're my new Gammy, and Mama said you're my new aunt?" Hazel asked Alexis.

Alexis nodded. This girl was too adorable. "You can call me Aunt Alexis," she said, but Hazel immediately began shaking her head.

"I don't like that name," Hazel said.

"Hazel May!" Lou reprimanded.

Hazel jumped at the stern tone of her mother's voice, but she didn't seem like she was going to take back her words. "Mama, I can't like that name. Alexis is the name of the person trying to make sure Uncle Jared won't marry Aunt Marsha again," she said.

Margie gasped but quickly stifled it.

Alexis felt her heart drop. She wanted to cover her eyes so that she didn't have to keep watching the scene playing out before her. Too bad this wasn't just a horror movie. This was her actual life.

"What in the world," Lou muttered. Then she moved Hazel so that she sat facing her. "Where on earth did you hear that?" Lou asked.

Hazel knew it was a time to be serious because she looked right into her mother's eyes as she said, "Brittany."

Alexis nodded. Jared's daughter. Jared's daughter with Marsha. Alexis didn't even need any more information to know where Brittany must've heard that.

"We're all supposed to hate Alexis," Hazel said innocently. "So I can't call my new aunt Alexis too."

Lou sighed, looking up at Alexis with a pity-filled gaze and then back at Hazel.

"Hazel, sweetie. Aunt Marsha and Uncle Jared are not going to get married again," Lou said slowly.

Hazel immediately began shaking her head. "That's not what Peter said."

Oh good. Jared's son was now involved as well.

Alexis suddenly felt the urge to laugh at this whole completely absurd situation. But then reality hit, and Alexis wanted to cry. Jared's kids hated her even before she'd met them. Watching her mother's own love story play out had proven just how hard it could be to overcome the hatred of grown children. But the hatred of two, young, impressionable kids whose whole world was their devoted father? Alexis felt a lump clog her throat.

"Peter said that Aunt Marsha wants to marry Uncle Jared again," Hazel corrected.

Lou shook her head. "What is my sister doing to those poor kids?" she asked, sounding a combination of angry and defeated.

"Hazel. Aunt Marsha doesn't want to be married to Uncle Jared. She's in love with her new boyfriend," Lou explained, trying to make sense of Marsha's complicated life in five-year-old terms.

"But she told Peter and Brittany she did want to marry him. She loves him, Mama. But Alexis . . ." Hazel said her name like a curse, and Alexis's heart cracked.

"Alexis is Uncle Jared's new girlfriend. He's dating her because Aunt Marsha asked Uncle Jared to not be married anymore," Lou said, sounding like she was hating having to make this clear to her little girl. A little girl too innocent to be dragged into all of this. But she was already there, so now Lou had to help her navigate.

"So Aunt Marsha is in love with her new boyfriend, and Uncle Jared is in love with Alexis?" Hazel asked, her head tilted to the side as she tried to comprehend what her mother was saying.

"Something like that," Lou said.

Hazel pursed her lips. "Well I think someone should tell Peter and Brittany that," she stated before looking up at Alexis.

"Okay, I can call you Aunt Alexis, and I can love you," Hazel declared as she stood and wrapped her little arms around Alexis's legs.

Thank heavens for that small comfort because, judging by this conversation, Alexis was in for a whole world of hurt.

CHAPTER SIX

"HELLO, MRS. HASKELL?" Olivia called out as she entered Dean's home.

Both Dean and his mother had insisted that Olivia no longer knock when she came into his house. He'd given her a key and let her know his home was her home, but she still felt weird entering the space, especially when she knew that Dean's mom was the only one home. Dean was working in Seattle that day and wouldn't be home for a few hours. But Olivia had been laden with Bess's newest experiments for the food truck when she'd gone over to drop off her most recent bookkeeping, and she knew she wanted to put most of the food in Dean's fridge.

Ever since Mrs. Haskell had moved in, Olivia and the girls would go over to Dean's home for meals and time together instead of the other way around. They wanted to make sure Mrs. Haskell felt as involved as possible, and moving their family events to Dean's house seemed like the right thing to do.

Loud barking and then the skittering of paws against the hardwood floors sounded, and Olivia grinned as she was greeted by Buster, Dean's beloved dog. Olivia bent over to give the cute dog some love before walking into the kitchen to drop off all the food. She heard Buster following her, and she guessed he was going to be her companion for the evening. At least until Dean came home. The dog really did love his dad most of all.

"Good afternoon, Olivia," Mrs. Haskell greeted when the two met in the kitchen.

Dean's state-of-the-art kitchen had kind of been wasted on the bachelor in the last few years since he'd moved back to Whisling. The previous owners had been avid cooks, and their stainless steel kitchen proved it. The white marble island and white countertops gave the nearly all silver room a welcome feel, as did the two big windows that allowed for a ton of light on the days that Whisling Island wasn't all gray and cloudy. Which wasn't today. It looked like a storm would be coming in soon. Olivia hoped Dean would be able to catch a ferry back from Seattle before it did.

"I just have some dishes from Bess and thought I'd stick them in here. Feel free to help yourself to anything that looks good," Olivia said. Then she turned to give her boyfriend's mom a smile after she'd put away all the food.

Mrs. Haskell was still too thin, a result of not eating well after her husband suddenly passed. But her cheeks weren't as sunken as they used to be, and she seemed to have some more color in her skin. When Mrs. Haskell had first moved back in with Dean, she'd been so pale that Pearl, Olivia's youngest, had almost commented on it. Thankfully Olivia had been able to get a hand over her daughter's mouth, and Dean had directed his mother's attention elsewhere.

Like Dean, his mother was taking it a day at a time after losing Mr. Haskell. She was eating better and had even started laughing again, typically at Olivia's daughters' antics. She still seemed fragile, yet so much stronger than a few short months before.

"Oh, that chicken looks quite nice," Mrs. Haskell said as she looked into the fridge Olivia was still holding open.

"I haven't tried it, but I'm sure it's delicious. I'm pretty sure my new sister-in-law is incapable of cooking anything short of spectacular," Olivia said, and Mrs. Haskell cracked a smile.

That was good news.

Olivia brought out the chicken for Mrs. Haskell and pushed it in her direction.

"Are your brother and his bride already back from their honeymoon?" Mrs. Haskell asked while she cut off a piece of chicken and began warming it in the microwave.

Olivia nodded.

"One week was as long as Bess could stay away from her truck," Olivia teased, and Mrs. Haskell chuckled as she took her plate of chicken out of the microwave.

Another sign of happiness. Man, Mrs. Haskell was really breaking through.

"Oh, this chicken is divine," Mrs. Haskell said as she pushed the takeout container holding the rest of the chicken toward Olivia. "Please try some."

Olivia wasn't exactly hungry, but she also would not make Mrs. Haskell eat alone if she didn't want to, so Olivia cut off a small portion and warmed it up.

"Oh, it really is good," Olivia said as she tried her piece. "Bess makes all the rest of us look bad with those cooking skills of hers," she said as she took another bite. She was nearly full, and yet she was thinking about cutting herself another portion, it was that delicious.

"Oh, but you've got your own incredible qualities, Olivia," Mrs. Haskell said with a soft smile. "I know a young man clearly smitten over you, and I can't blame him one bit."

Olivia grinned. She had hoped that Dean's mom liked her; it

had always seemed so. But this was the first verbal assurance she'd been given, and man did it feel good.

"Thank you, Tina," Olivia murmured as her cheeks burned bright red. She didn't know what else to say, so she hoped those simple words were enough to convey her gratitude for Tina's comment. It really meant the world to her that Dean's mom thought highly of her.

"It's the truth," Mrs. Haskell said, returning Olivia's smile.

A commotion at the front door and Buster's race to see who it was let the women know someone had joined them. Olivia would put money down that it was her girls. She'd told them she'd be back to their cottage in just a few minutes, but Olivia was going to guess they'd gotten hungry for treats—the way ten- and twelve-year-old children always seemed to. And Mrs. Haskell loved to spoil her girls with whatever sweets she had on hand.

"Mom?" Dean called out, and Olivia's eyes went wide with surprise. Dean was supposed to be in Seattle for a few more hours.

Mrs. Haskell's eyes darted from Olivia toward the front door.

"I'm in the kitchen with Olivia, dear," she called out to her son, smiling widely at Olivia.

Okay. That seemed a little bit weird. It was almost as if Mrs. Haskell was alerting Dean to Olivia's presence. Olivia might not live in the home, but she had been assured she was welcome to join them anytime she wanted.

Dean and Buster joined them nearly immediately, the former shaking off the remnants of the raindrops that were still in his hair. He must've been wearing a coat, though, because his clothes were completely dry.

"You're back early," Olivia said as she gave Dean a chaste kiss. They tried to keep their PDA to a minimum, especially in front of Mrs. Haskell and Olivia's girls. She was pretty sure the three females were all in firm agreement that they liked her and Dean together, but she didn't want to push any boundaries or make anyone feel uncomfortable. She assumed maybe they'd up their PDA one day, after they were engaged or something, but for now, quick kisses would have to do in front of others.

"I was hoping to beat the storm. All the plans I had for the rest of the day were cancelled due to weather," Dean said.

Mrs. Haskell gasped, and both Olivia and Dean turned to look at her. Olivia swore she saw Dean glare at his mother out of the corner of her eye. What was going on? Sure, Dean's work was important, but the gasp was a bit much for some cancelled meetings.

"I just know you were supposed to be entertaining that really important client this evening," Mrs. Haskell said, and Olivia nodded, beginning to understand. She hadn't known Dean's evening plans were with one of his biggest clients.

"Yeah," Dean muttered, dropping his eyes to the ground, and Olivia wondered who this client was. Was the meeting really that big of a deal?

"Can you reschedule for tomorrow?" Olivia asked.

Dean shook his head. "This storm isn't supposed to blow over for a few more days," he said.

Olivia pursed her lips. "So it's safer to stay on the island," she said, and Dean nodded.

The ferry traveled in the rain. If it didn't, it would hardly ever move. But Olivia knew that every time one took the ferry during a storm, they were taking the chance that they might get stranded. Because when storms got too rough, the ferry cancelled its passages.

"I'm sure whoever the client is will be understanding," Olivia said with a smile.

"Oh, I know she will be. That's part of why this is so frustrating. I was just . . . I really wanted this meeting to happen," Dean said.

Olivia moved in so that she could give her boyfriend a hug. She wasn't sure she was understanding everything, but she hated that Dean was so upset.

"You can go back to Seattle in a few days," Olivia said into Dean's chest as he wrapped his arms around her. His chin dropped to the top of her head, and Olivia tightened her grip on Dean. She knew they typically limited their PDA, but this was okay, right? It was a hug of comfort. Except when Dean started rubbing her back and then dropped a kiss onto her head. Olivia ached to turn up and capture his lips but was very much aware that Dean's mother was standing right behind her.

"Oh the heck with it," Dean said as he let go of Olivia and took a few steps back. He paced one way and then the other, dipping and then raising his head. "Let's go take a walk on our beach."

Olivia cocked her head in confusion as she watched the erratic motions of her boyfriend. Why was he being so weird? But then again, Olivia would never turn down a walk on the beach with Dean, even in this weather. One didn't grow up on Whisling without learning how to weather a few storms. Even one as bad as this one. With the right jacket and pair of boots, the rain would be kind of fun to walk in. At least for a few minutes before the cold set in.

"Sure," Olivia said as she moved to the door. She'd have to run home for her best raincoat and change into her boots, but that could be fun. Especially if it would take Dean's mind off his missed meeting.

"No, you stay here. I'll grab your rain items so you don't get soaked running to the cottage, and I'll bring the girls with me so they can stay here with Mom." Dean looked to his mom who nodded along with his plan.

"Oh, there's no need for that. The girls will be fine on their own for a few more minutes," Olivia said, not wanting to inconvenience Dean's mom.

But Mrs. Haskell shook her head. "I'll just be warming up some of this food from Bess for dinner. It will be nice to have the company," she said.

Olivia grinned and nodded. She figured she couldn't argue with that. She turned to tell Dean where she kept her jacket and boots but saw that he'd already left. The door suddenly slamming and Buster returning to the kitchen told Olivia she'd missed Dean by seconds. Why was he in such a hurry?

Olivia figured he was still a little off from having his day cut short and his meetings cancelled. She knew he took his work seriously, even if he worked way less than he had when he'd lived in Portland. But he liked to do his best work for anyone who hired him. And maybe cutting his day short, thanks to the storm, made Dean feel like he was selling his clients short? Which would be ridiculous but something she could imagine Dean worrying about.

"Should we start getting that dinner ready while we wait?" Olivia asked as Buster walked circles around her legs.

But instead of responding, Mrs. Haskell got right to work taking delectable fare out of the fridge and prepping them for the oven or stove, depending on how the dishes would best be warmed. The meal was a bit of a hodgepodge since it was full of different components Bess had been testing, but they'd been given these types of leftovers enough times before that Olivia knew none of them minded the mishmash, especially when it was Bess doing the cooking.

"Oh this soup smells delicious," Mrs. Haskell said as she poured an herby mixture into a pot. Buster barked, as if adding his agreement.

Olivia grinned at the dog before responding to Dean's mom.

"It's a blend of Italian wedding soup and chicken noodle," she relayed. "Bess has been working on getting the ingredient ratios just right for a few weeks now. She wants details on what we think of that one."

Mrs. Haskell nodded. "Judging by the smell, I'd say she's got it just right."

Olivia didn't doubt it. Even though Bess acted worried about some of her dishes, Olivia knew that Bess didn't often allow others to taste her stuff unless she was already sure of their outstanding quality. Olivia was pretty sure Bess just needed reassurance before selling her experiments on her truck, and Olivia and her family were more than happy to give it.

Buster's sudden bark and dash to the front door told Olivia Dean was already back.

"It's so cold," Olivia heard her Pearl say as the front door opened, followed by lots of stomping. Olivia was grateful that her girls were working to clean off their shoes before coming further into the home. Even though the distance between her cottage and Dean's house was short, thanks to the hundreds of leaves that littered their backyard at this time of year, it was easy to get some muck on one's shoes quite quickly.

"I think I have a leaf in my hair," Rachel said. "Do I have a leaf in my hair?" Rachel asked either Dean or Pearl.

Pearl immediately began laughing and even Dean chuckled a bit before saying, "Just a couple."

"There are like ten," Pearl said. "I told you to put on your hood."

Pearl soon joined the women in the kitchen, still laughing at her sister who she'd left behind. Olivia was guessing Dean was helping with the leaf situation.

"Hey, Pearly," Mrs. Haskell said immediately.

Pearl rushed into the hug of the woman who had become a staple in Dean's home and, therefore, in Pearl's life.

"Hi," Pearl said from within her hug, and she somehow came away with a piece of chocolate in her hand. Where had Mrs. Haskell gotten the treat? And how had the handoff been made? Olivia swore if drug deals were left to grandmothers and grand-children, no one would ever get caught.

Pearl then turned her attention to Olivia, smiling largely and just staring at her mom.

"Pearl?" Olivia asked, looking her daughter over to make sure everything was okay. Sure Pearl smiled a lot, but this goofy grin was a little strange. "Why are you smiling like that?"

"She's just happy, Mom," Rachel said as she finally joined them in the kitchen, a tiny piece of brown leaf and a few rain-drops in her auburn hair the only evidence of her hoodless adventure. "Can't she be happy?"

"Yes, of course, but—" Olivia began when Dean wrapped his arms around her waist from behind, stealing her train of thought.

"So that walk?" Dean asked, and Olivia nodded before turning toward him.

He dropped his arms, and Olivia immediately yearned for them again. But they couldn't very well leave the house all wrapped up together, could they?

She took her jacket from him before kicking off her tennis shoes and putting on the rain boots Dean had brought back for her.

"You ready to brave this rain together?" Dean asked.

Olivia nodded, loving the way he'd said *together*. Honestly, there wasn't much in the world Olivia wasn't ready to brave as long as Dean was with her.

"Have fun!" Pearl called out, and Olivia swore she heard the thud of Rachel hitting Pearl. But when she looked back at her girls and Dean's mom, they all just beamed back at her as if nothing was wrong. Maybe Olivia had imagined the noise?

There was no way Rachel could've hit Pearl that hard without Pearl tattling.

Olivia glanced up at Dean, but he seemed to be oblivious as well. Maybe it was all in her head?

Dean took her hand and popped a huge umbrella open over their heads as they walked out into the rain.

It wasn't as bad as Olivia had imagined. Typically, the wind and rain had to be torrential for the ferry to stop running. Olivia didn't know if it was just a lull in the storm or if the storm was already on its way out, but either way, Olivia would take it. Because even though the rain was coming down in sheets, it wasn't blowing sideways due to the gentle winds. So between her boots and long jacket, Olivia was pretty well protected from the brunt of it.

"Do you remember the first time we remet?" Dean asked as they walked down the rocks from Dean's backyard and onto the coarse, beige sand, pulling Olivia away from her thoughts of the storm.

"Of course," she said, easily remembering the evening that she'd sat with Dean on this sand. The night had been clear, unlike this one, and it had been beautiful. Olivia had been right in the thick of her divorce fallout. She'd needed a friend, and that was exactly what Dean had been for so long. She remembered the way tiny butterflies had excited her, but it had been too soon to feel something for a new man. And although she'd known that, it had been fun to feel that instant attraction. The butterflies that now resided in her belly were the adult version of those tiny flittings, and thanks to Dean once again wrapping her up in his free arm, they were going into a frantic tizzy.

"Ever since that day, I've thought of this as our beach," Dean said.

Olivia nodded. She felt the same way. It was kind of funny

that neither had said the words aloud until that moment, but it was an amusing discovery.

"I remember when I saw you standing right there . . ." Dean said, pointing to the spot where he'd first seen Olivia. Dean had left the island for college and hadn't come back until a few years after a divorce of his own. His hadn't been quite as intense as Olivia's, but it hadn't been pleasant—it was still a divorce, after all—and he'd been battling his own demons when they'd first sat there on that beach.

"For a second I wondered if you were real. You were a literal vision. You've always been the most beautiful woman I've ever known . . ." Dean said, alluding to the crush he'd had on Olivia back in high school before she'd started dating her ex-husband, Bart.

"But then you started speaking, and I began to realize your outer beauty paled in comparison to the woman you are right here." Dean tapped lightly just above Olivia's heart, and she turned so that she could face him. She didn't like that they weren't having this conversation face to face.

As she turned, Dean peeked out from under the umbrella. Seemingly satisfied that the rain wasn't coming down too hard, he closed the umbrella and enveloped Olivia in both of his arms, allowing her to burrow into his warmth. She would take a Dean hug over an umbrella any day.

Olivia carefully glanced up at Dean with one eye, worried that the rain would nearly drown her face if she looked fully upward. But the rain was dying down quickly, and when Olivia took her peek, it was just tiny droplets that greeted her. She was suddenly grateful she'd decided to go sans makeup that morning. The rain would've made her an instant raccoon.

"You'd been hurt. You might've even felt a little broken. I won't deny that," Dean said.

Olivia thought back to those days right after Bart. She'd

been more than a little broken. She'd been a shell, hollow for fear that any type of feeling would be used against her.

"But you were still such a beacon. I knew I shouldn't have bothered you that night—you were so deep in your own thoughts—but I couldn't help it. My feet were drawn to you of their own accord. I haven't been able to stay away ever since," Dean said.

Olivia grinned. And wasn't she grateful for that.

"Olivia, I've loved you for a very long time. Maybe what I felt for you in high school wasn't true love yet, but to that seventeen-year-old boy, it was all consuming. Just like the love I have for you now. The love that we now share," he said.

Olivia pressed a kiss to Dean's lips in response. She wasn't sure what to say to such gorgeous words. Dean was the one who could speak his mind. Olivia was better at showing her love. So that's what she tried to do.

"It was a long road to each other," Dean said before Olivia added, "Too long."

Dean chuckled, and Olivia was grateful she'd thought of one good thing to say.

"Way too long. My best days have been the ones walking side by side with you," Dean said before letting go of Olivia.

What was he doing? Why was he letting go? Olivia had planned on kissing this man senseless in about point two seconds.

Dean dropped to one knee.

Oh my heavens. Dean just dropped to a knee.

Olivia felt her entire body cover with goosebumps as she watched the man she loved kneel there in the wet sand.

"What are you doing?" Olivia somehow managed to croak as she felt the urges to both laugh and cry.

"Olivia Penn. Will you do me the grand honor of being my wife? From now until forever more?" Dean had said the most beautiful words Olivia could've imagined, and she wanted to blurt out *yes*. But would just a normal *yes* suffice in a situation like this?

Dean pulled out a velvet box from his pocket, revealing the most beautiful teardrop-shaped diamond set on a thin gold band. Between the magnificent words and the spectacular ring, Olivia was completely stunned.

"Yes! A thousand times yes!" she blurted before covering her mouth and looking down at a now-laughing Dean.

"Did you just quote that Austen movie?" Dean asked.

Olivia felt her cheeks burn up even as she shook her head no. How could she have bungled the situation so badly, quoting one of the most memorable lines from one of the most memorable movies of all time. Dean had lobbed the ball, giving her a perfect proposal. All Olivia would've had to do was swing to knock it out of the park. Instead, she'd struck out.

"It's a good quote," Dean said with a giant grin as he slipped the ring on Olivia's finger before standing and gathering her in his arms. "Especially because you said my very favorite word. *Yes.*"

"I just wanted to match the beauty of your words, and it's all that came to me—"

"It was perfect," Dean said before capturing Olivia's lips, causing her to completely forget her name much less the embarrassment she'd just caused herself.

"I'd love to stand here celebrating like this all day, but you are shivering," Dean said as he pulled Olivia closer to him.

Was she shaking? She hadn't even noticed.

"It's not that cold," Olivia said through chattering teeth that she tried to calm with no luck.

Dean chuckled. "You're a fighter. Have I told you recently how much I admire you?"

"I mean, that proposal was pretty adequate. But you

could've talked a bit more about how you admire me," Olivia teased, her teeth still chattering.

Dean laughed again and pulled Olivia close to him as they hurried back along the beach toward his house.

They were both still laughing as they ran through the front door, but Olivia somehow remembering to stomp her shoes even though all she wanted to do was rush to her girls.

"Do they know?" Olivia asked as Dean helped her take her jacket off.

"Did you see Pearl's grin before we left?" Dean asked.

Olivia giggled once again. She honestly felt as if nothing in the world could touch her while she was on this magical high. And now she understood why her girls had been acting so strangely. Along with Mrs. Haskell. Slowly, the entire evening was beginning to make much more sense.

"Mom!" Pearl squealed as she slid through the foyer and right into Olivia's arms, followed closely by Rachel. They were all about to be steamrolled by Buster when Dean intervened, calling the dog toward his direction.

"You're getting married," Rachel said, her eyes a little red. Had her baby girl been crying?

"Is that okay?" Olivia asked, even though it tore her up to even ask the question. If Rachel said *no*, well, then Olivia would have found the one thing that could bring her right back down to earth.

"It's more than okay, Mom. We love Dean. And we love Dean for you. He makes you so happy. Happier than you've ever been," Rachel said, sending streams of tears down Olivia's cheeks. These poor girls had witnessed much too much in their short years. Especially Rachel. They hadn't lived with Bart in over four years, and the time had healed a lot for them, but Olivia had a feeling Rachel would never forget.

"Can I see the ring?" Pearl asked, and Olivia pushed out her hand, both girls grasping either side of it.

"Oh, it's so pretty," Pearl gushed as Rachel just stared.

"What do you think?" Olivia asked Rachel. She had a feeling this day was hitting her oldest harder than Olivia could imagine, and she wanted to be sure to be sensitive to that. Pearl had always been her light-hearted girl, lifting any situation, but Rachel was more level-headed, always serious.

"I had a dream that you and Dean were getting married," Rachel said quietly, and Olivia knew better than to say anything right then.

"This is the ring you wore at your wedding, Mom," Rachel said, finally meeting Olivia's eyes.

Olivia worked hard to not start crying again, but her emotions were at an all-time high. Granted, they were mostly good, but she knew she and Rachel were still letting go of some of the very last remnants of the bad.

"That's unbelievable," Olivia finally said.

Rachel nodded. "I know. I think I was supposed to have that dream. So that I wouldn't be scared at all about a man joining our lives again."

Olivia crushed her oldest to her chest. Rachel felt emotions beyond her years, in some ways experiencing too much. But Olivia was so grateful for this tender mercy that could only come from God. And Olivia felt the dream had been for her too. Because now she felt like she truly deserved this new beginning.

Pearl joined in on their hug, and Olivia glanced up to see Dean holding his mother.

The five of them had been through a lot. Divorces and, more recently, death. But they were holding on to one another. They were moving forward together. And because of that, their future was bright.

CHAPTER SEVEN

JULIA SAT up suddenly in her bed, memories of her most recent nightmare plaguing her even in the morning light. She quickly rubbed the sleep from her eyes, knowing that, despite her fear, she was safe.

In order to seek comfort, Julia looked to her phone to see the words Ellis sent a variation of every morning. *Good morning, Darlin'*, this morning's text read. Julia held her phone to her chest. Man, she missed him.

But Ellis had had to go back on tour. He'd talked about cancelling it to stay with Julia, but she'd assured him that was crazy talk. His fans, his band, and so many more people were counting on him to finish what he'd said he'd do. To quit midway for Julia when they were . . . well, she and Ellis were still nothing, as far as she knew.

She liked him. And she knew he liked her. But no promises had been made before he'd left. Because there were no promises to make. Julia wasn't sure she was the kind of woman who could really love. She had fifty years of experience telling her just how little she understood that emotion.

One of the security officers who'd come up to check on

things after the stalker breach had stayed with Julia. In her home. And she hated it.

This man who she didn't know at all had free range of her home. And even though Julia trusted the company he worked for, she didn't know him from Adam. But he was there, night and day. Just steps from Julia at all times. In the name of protecting her. It was all bizarre.

Julia walked to her closet, pulling on a sweater and a comfy pair of jeans. She'd showered the night before in an attempt to calm her racing thoughts and get herself sleepy. It hadn't worked. All she had to show for it now was crazy bedhead because she'd tried to sleep with wet hair.

Julia glanced warily at her reflection. Yes, it was as bad as she'd assumed, so she pulled her hair back in a ponytail and put on some minimal makeup. It wasn't like she was going anywhere.

She and Dax's team had come up with a security plan after the stalker had struck. Since everyone was on high alert, they decided that along with a full-time guard, Julia should leave the home only when necessary. And they'd just allow people through her gates who'd been vetted by her security agency. So basically, Julia's entire life was taking place within the walls of her compound. For who knew how long.

It was only when Dax had come home from his honeymoon a few days earlier that Julia had felt able to air her concerns. She'd told Dax about her dislike of having a man she didn't know living with her, and Dax's suggestion had been to get to know the man.

Julia had barked out a loud laugh at that one. Dax hadn't met the goliath of a man who'd been sent to guard her, but Julia was pretty sure the man had to pay for every word he spoke. Of course she'd tried to get to know him. Every question had been answered with a single word, if not a grunt. Yeah, he wasn't there to make friends. Dax had softened at Julia's words and said he'd see what he could do.

Julia hated that she was bringing Dax more problems right after he'd been married, but the man had called her to check in. He'd actually called her before that, from his honeymoon, when he'd heard about the stalker incident. But Julia had hung up on him. She thought Bess would appreciate that. So when Dax called after the honeymoon, Julia felt it was her responsibility to put his worries at ease. Even though, technically, they were just client and manager, she knew over the years she and Dax and Bess had formed a friendship. Dax had begun the phone call by telling Julia the call had been demanded by Bess. Julia didn't doubt it. Bess was the kind of woman to put the needs of another before her own.

So Julia had voiced her complaints to Dax, and she figured he'd have it all worked out soon. The man was a magician when it came to these kinds of matters.

Thinking of you. Julia texted the words she would've never had the courage to say aloud.

Did you have that same nightmare? Ellis responded almost immediately.

It's fine. I'm fine.

Julia wanted to reassure him. She didn't want him worrying about her while he was in the middle of a huge tour. But according to Ellis, his thoughts were often on Julia, so of course he worried about her. Especially while the stalker was still at large. He still talked about cancelling the rest of his tour at least a few times a week.

You're incredible.

I don't know about that, but go on.

Julia smiled, loving the confidence Ellis gave her. The way she was with Ellis was different. She felt admired, but somehow she knew he didn't admire her in the way other men in her life had. He knew her. And what he didn't know, he wanted to get to know. Ellis wanted to dig deep while others had just wanted a shallow version of her. And that was one of the reasons Julia kept moving forward with him. Although she still felt scared that she was incapable of the kind of real love a relationship between a man and a woman needed, with Ellis she had hope that maybe she could develop that capability. And that thought was equal parts amazing and intimidating.

You are kind, loyal, beautiful, smart, funny, quick witted, and maybe most of all, you are incredibly brave.

Julia leaned against the doorway of her bedroom which she had been just about to leave; Ellis's words had rendered her incapable of moving forward. She hadn't imagined anyone would ever see all of that in her. She felt compelled to tell Ellis what she felt about him.

You're open, truthful, have a poetic way with words. You're good to the core, and you make me laugh. You are capable, incredibly sexy, and a perfect gentleman.

Julia stared at her phone as she watched those three dots blink, wondering if she'd come on too strong. But it was the truth, and with Ellis, she felt she could be honest.

I hope I'm not always a perfect gentleman.

Julia laughed as another text came in.

I didn't say those things about you for you to return them, but thank you. To know that a woman who means so much to me thinks so highly of me? That's a gift. This tour couldn't end soon enough.

Julia's heart flipped as she considered those words. The tour being done meant Ellis returning. That still wouldn't be for a few more months, but the fact that he'd gone again and still wanted to return to Whisling? The excitement helped her forget her current problems.

I have to run into a meeting, but I'll text you later. Take care, Julia.

Julia's eyes lingered on those last words. Ellis was always sure to end any text conversation with something to let Julia know he cared about her. Were they moving forward? What was the next step for them? Julia realized those were questions for another day because for the next few months while Ellis was on tour, things had to stay the same. She didn't want to add any unnecessary pressure to his already full plate.

Julia slipped her phone into her back pocket as she padded down to her kitchen—choosing to stay bare-footed while at home —and began searching through her fridge for some breakfast. It was grocery delivery day so she was light on produce, knocking oatmeal off the list of breakfast possibilities. Julia wasn't a huge fan of oats and could only stomach them when they were loaded with fruit. A lack of fruit also kept Julia from being able to make an acai bowl, another breakfast staple for her, so she stuck with eggs. One couldn't go wrong with a plate of eggs.

Julia pulled them out, along with a bag of shredded cheese. She was cracking open her first egg when Stan, her bodyguard, came to stand next to a nearby window. "Stan the silent man" was the moniker Julia used in her mind for the hulking guard.

"Would you like some eggs?" Julia offered, and when no sound came from his direction, she had to look up to see him shaking his head.

Julia nodded. That was fine with her. She didn't make the best eggs anyway.

She cracked her second egg before mixing them in a bowl with some cheese and then pouring the mixture into a sizzling pan. Julia had read somewhere to make eggs low and slow, but she never had the patience for that. Besides, Julia really didn't mind a rubbery egg. She knew she was in a minority.

She scrambled her eggs quickly and was pouring them onto a plate when the doorbell rang. She tensed up for a moment. If someone was ringing her doorbell, that meant they'd been let in through the gate. But she hadn't approved any visitors. Which meant either someone had breached her outer security or Stan had let her visitor in.

She looked over at Stan who seemed unalarmed. Well, that was a good sign. But what to do now?

"Can I get that?" Julia asked, just making sure.

Stan grunted in what Julia assumed was the affirmative. She guessed this meant the guest at the door had been vetted. Stan the silent man and his lack of communication were going to be the death of her.

Julia moved slowly toward the door so that Stan could stop her if need be, but she got all the way to the door without getting tackled to the ground. Again, another good sign.

She shook off the feeling of fear and hurt that consumed her every time she walked through her foyer. She hated that someone had come into her safe space and that she and her security team still had no idea why the person had broken in. Who had taken such a risk for a flower and a note? And why? Julia had a feeling the person had wanted to show her how susceptible she was to him. Well, mission accomplished. Except Julia would never voice the words aloud. She would never admit defeat. Even if she shook as she stood in her own home. She knew others from Stan's team were working to discover who the stalker was. The person would be behind bars soon. But Julia had a feeling her house wouldn't feel like her home again until after he was.

She opened the door, her jaw dropping, before quickly gathering herself.

"I guess we didn't have to wait fifteen years this time

around," Julia said to the man at her door, shaking her head that Liam had once again shown up out of the blue.

"Judging by your expression, Stan didn't relay the message that I'd be joining you today?" Liam asked.

Julia shook her head. "Stan isn't exactly the chatty type," she said as she nodded toward where she'd left Stan in the kitchen.

"Huh. We had a lovely conversation," Liam said.

Julia narrowed her eyes. "Did you just use *lovely* in everyday dialogue?" she asked, unsure if she was more perplexed by that or by Stan's ability to have a lovely conversation.

"I did. Don't you?" Liam asked, and it was only then that Julia looked down to see two bags at Liam's feet. Bags that looked suspiciously like luggage.

"What are you doing here?" Julia asked, her eyes traveling from the bags back to Liam's face.

"Stan didn't tell you about that either?" Liam asked.

Julia raised her arms in defeat. "Let's assume Stan has told me nothing." Which was exactly how much he'd told her.

"Dax hired me," Liam said, and Julia let her eyes go wide to show that that one sentence still explained nothing.

"He knew you wanted someone in your home who you knew but who would also be capable of protecting you," Liam continued.

Julia nodded. So far she was following. But how had Dax found Liam? "He saw that we worked together for Ally."

Right. Of course. Liam had trained Julia for the spy and stunt work for her hit television show. Julia knew Dax was good at what he did. It made sense that he'd found that connection.

"So why are you here?" Julia asked.

Dax trying to hire Liam made sense. The man was practically a legend in the spy world. He could probably guard the president with his background. And yet he was here.

"Julia, after Dax told me about your stalker, I was on the first flight out here," Liam said, so much about what he said shocking her.

"Why?" was the only question Julia could manage.

"I've known you practically my whole life. We're friends," Liam finally stated.

Julia knew she wore a look of astonishment that conveyed what she felt. Were they friends? Sure, they'd known one another for years. But Julia hadn't been joking about not seeing Liam for fifteen years. After Julia declared her love for Liam in high school, the next time she saw him was about fifteen years later, when he'd been hired as her trainer for Ally. And then another fifteen years later, they'd run into one another at a diner a few months back. Liam had helped her repair her relationship with some of her family members. Julia guessed friends did that. But she also supposed friends spoke to one another more often than every fifteen years.

"Friends," Julia finally said, as if the word was foreign to her. But the fact was, even if Liam was only a partial friend, he was a better alternative to Stan the silent man. So Julia opened her door wider to let Liam in.

Liam was coming into her house. With luggage. Liam was staying at her house. Julia shook her head. Of course he was. This was so perfectly normal in their relationship.

"Are you okay?" Liam asked as he closed the door behind him, and Julia shrugged, trying to look anywhere but at the ground where the stalker had left the rose.

"I saw the pictures . . . anyway, let's get you out of here," he said as he ushered Julia up the stairs.

He knew. He understood that the stalker had been in her foyer and the place made her feel uneasy. Maybe it wouldn't be terrible to have him around.

"So you'll be staying here?" Julia asked as she led Liam down her hall. She wasn't sure where she was taking him until she asked for more direction.

"I'll be taking Stan's place," Liam said.

Julia's eyes went wide. She'd thought surely Liam was an addition to the team. Not the whole team. Her heart began to pound against her chest. Liam was going to be staying with her. In her home. Alone.

No big deal. Stan the silent man had done the same for weeks now. Julia just had to pretend that Liam was like Stan. But as she glanced back and watched Liam's easy saunter, she realized pretending he was the silent, hulking Stan was going to be difficult. Nope, more than difficult. Practically impossible.

Julia frowned as she got to the doorway of the room Stan had been using. It was on the same level as Julia's but down the hall quite a ways. She hadn't felt comfortable having Stan any nearer to her.

Once they got to Stan's open door, sure enough, there he stood packing up his stuff. He'd definitely known what was happening. He just hadn't seen the need to relay any of it to Julia.

She shifted so that her frown could now be sent at the silent man. Couldn't he have given her the tiniest heads-up?

Stan seemed, as always, to not care what Julia was doing. Granted, it wasn't his job to care about what she was doing, just that she was safe. But the lack of care still annoyed the crap out of her. They'd had to live together for the last two weeks. The least he could've done was tried to have a conversation. Even just one.

"There have been no further sightings of the stalker. I'll have my phone on me if you need any other updates." Silent Stan was silent no more. Seriously? Two sentences just because he could now speak to Liam?

Now that Stan had finally spoken, Julia wondered if she'd gleaned a little more insight into why the man had always been so silent. He'd emphasized the word *stalker* with a tone that could only be described as apathetic, making it sound as if he wasn't sure such a being existed. Telling Julia that he probably thought she was some stuck-up, has-been diva who'd been dying for attention so had made up some stalker. She knew she was assuming a lot, but it wasn't just this conversation that was giving her this impression. It was amazing what silence could say. And Stan had said a lot with his silence over the weeks. Well, thank heavens the silent man would be leaving soon. Julia didn't want the man guarding her to not even believe the stalker existed. What kind of danger did that leave her in?

Her anger and frustration at the past two weeks began to well up within her, and suddenly she felt a calming hand on the small of her back.

"Do you want to go rest in your room for a minute? Stan will be gone soon, and then you can give me the lay of the land," Liam offered.

Julia let out a whoosh of breath, grateful she hadn't been allowed to give the silent man a piece of her mind. It really would've been too much. And then he would've gone back to his buddies at the security office with tales that Julia Price really was as terrible as they'd all assumed. Julia didn't want to burn that bridge. And she was grateful Liam had been there to keep her from doing just that.

She slid past Liam, careful not to touch any part of herself to him. Her back still felt warm where he'd touched her, and Julia didn't need that kind of confusion in her life.

When she got to her room, she closed the door behind her, soundlessly taking in her all-white oasis. She loved this room. But more than just the furnishings and plush pillows and comforter, the best part was the view. The vast blue ocean stood before her, full of possibilities and shadows. It was equal parts exhilarating and terrifying. Julia loved that about the island.

Still feeling the chill that had invaded her in the foyer, Julia got back into bed, curling up under her covers. Finally feeling safe and secure again, the pang in Julia's stomach reminded her her eggs were now very cold and congealed. She'd have to figure out something else to eat for breakfast later.

Julia thought about pulling her phone out of her pocket to scan social media or her email but instead decided to lay there in complete peace and solitude. There was something powerful about being alone. When one chose to be alone. When the state was inflicted on Julia, it didn't feel quite the same way. But right now, she could be with Liam or Stan the silent man. Yet she was choosing not to. She was choosing this place in her bed, and Julia liked the piece of ownership that that one action brought.

She needed to do more things like this for herself. Her stomach growled once again.

But after breakfast.

She crawled back out of her bed, this time opting to leave it unmade. Making her bed every morning had become part of her routine here on Whisling. Something she hadn't done since her days in the rat hole in LA where she'd resided before getting her big break. She'd always had housekeepers to do those jobs for her since then. And although she had a woman come in and clean every couple of days here on Whisling—Julia knew her strengths, and cleaning surely wasn't one of them—her house cleaner didn't come in daily so Julia had fallen into the habit again. One she liked a lot. But since she'd already made her bed that morning and was about to faint from hunger, she decided to leave it and get to the important stuff. Food.

Julia had always loved breakfast. While many actresses kept their bellies empty, especially on mornings when they had to shoot, Julia couldn't. Well, she could've, but she never wanted to. Yes, her size zero jeans would always fit a bit snugger after eating a meal, but Julia figured she'd given up so much in the food category for her career that breakfast was a sacrifice she wasn't willing to make. So when she'd retired and moved to Whisling, breakfast had become more than a meal. And it couldn't be missed without dire consequences . . . which were setting in now. She was feeling a little bit faint and a lotta bit cranky. She needed food, and she needed it stat.

When Julia had first decided she was okay with gaining some weight after her retirement, the main place she'd upped her caloric intake was breakfast. She'd started eating French toast drenched in syrup or bacon, eggs, and toast. But after a couple weeks of those indulgent meals every day, Julia began to tire of the lethargy that would set in after those enormous breakfasts. So she started opting for the lighter meals she now ate. But that didn't make breakfast any less of a tradition.

When Julia got to the kitchen, her first item of business was getting rid of the cold eggs. She thought about starting a new batch, but they just didn't sound as good as they had an hour before. So she dug around a bit more before finding a loaf of bread. She began to toast two pieces before getting out some butter and grape jelly to slather on. There was something about melting butter and grape jelly melding together, yum.

"Stan said you'd be down here," Liam spoke, and his voice nearly made Julia jump. She wasn't used to having conversation in her home.

"Did he?" Julia asked, feeling surprised that Stan knew her so well. Granted, he'd been following her around for fourteen days. She figured it made sense that he would. But because she knew so little about him, the thought wasn't a comforting one.

"He let me know that you aren't ever quite yourself until you've had breakfast," Liam added with a grin.

Liam grinning. Okay, that was new. Maybe he really

wanted to start this client/bodyguard relationship on the right foot. Because that's what this was. Liam wasn't here because he wanted to see Julia. He'd talked about friendship, but this wasn't a friendly visit. Liam was here in a professional capacity, and although Julia's childhood crush begged her to do anything but stay professional, she knew it was necessary. Besides, she had Ellis now. Although she had no idea what she had with Ellis. When had her life become a soap opera?

"He's right," Julia said as she caught the toast as it popped out of the toaster and then began making a beautiful concoction of bread, melty butter, and gooey jelly.

Julia crunched down on her toast before realizing Stan had never partaken in meals with her—she honestly had no idea when Stan had eaten—but maybe Liam would want to.

"Do you want some?" Julia asked around a mouthful of toast. Cute. Not that she wanted to impress Liam. Okay, maybe she wanted to impress Liam a little. Didn't every woman want the guy who'd once turned them down to regret it? But not impress him so much that he wanted her now. Julia knew one thing for sure when it came to Liam. Any real feelings she'd felt for him were in her distant past. Weren't they?

"I mean, not this piece," Julia said when her mouth was clear of food. "I can make you your own piece of toast."

Liam chuckled as he shook his head. "Thanks for the offer, but I got something on the way here."

Duh. Liam had to have been up for hours if he'd arrived on Whisling from who-knew-where by nine am.

"But if the offer stands on whatever you eat for lunch, I'd love some. I typically don't eat with my clients," that explained the silent man's absence during meals, "but we're friends," Liam said as Julia stuffed in another bite of toast because, honestly, she wasn't sure what to say to that. Did Liam know what a friend was? Granted, Julia was just truly learning the definition of the word herself. The people she'd thought were her friends in LA hadn't really been. It was only after coming to Whisling that she'd been blessed with true friendship. At least as an adult. She'd had a few true friends growing up in Travers, all of whom she'd lost touch with over the years because she hadn't continued being a very good friend to them.

"You keep calling us friends," Julia said after she'd taken several swigs from her tumbler of water.

"Isn't that what you'd call us?" Liam asked.

Julia shook her head, deciding it was time to be fully honest with Liam. She'd begun tearing down the walls of perfection she'd once used to impress everyone while on her last trip home to Travers. But this was going to be even more than that. It had to be if they were going to live together. So ready or not, honest Julia was coming out.

"I'd say I had a crush on you back in high school. You rejected me. We then didn't talk for years until you trained me for Ally where you pretended you didn't know me and I let you pretend. Fast forward fifteen years and you show up at a diner where I happen to be eating and give me advice that changes my life. Now, a few months later, you're in my house as my bodyguard. Definitely not a typical friendship," she said, feeling relieved she'd let that all out. She felt a tiny bit of the embarrassment she'd anticipated, but mostly she just felt grateful she could tell Liam the whole truth. At least the way she saw the truth. She'd learned from her relationship with her family that sometimes one person's truth wasn't the same as another's.

"So an atypical friendship then," Liam said.

Julia fought the urge to blow out a sigh of frustration. Why was Liam so intent on sticking with this phrasing? Unless . . . was he worried Julia still had feelings for him? Nearly forty years after the fact? Julia felt her cheeks flame. Okay, this was really embarrassing.

"I don't still have a crush on you," she blurted out, her cheeks growing redder. She'd only promised herself she'd be honest. She'd said nothing to herself about keeping her dignity.

"Um, I didn't think . . . did I say anything . . ." Liam stammered.

Julia wished she could just melt into a puddle of her own shame. Had she really just said that aloud? This whole conversation was heading south, sounding very much like the dialogue of teens, not fifty-somethings. Julia should be beyond conversations like this, shouldn't she?

"I felt like you were carefully placing me in the friend zone when you kept on saying *friend*," Julia said. Might as well keep up her honesty. It was working so well for her. "I just didn't want you to feel the need to be so careful."

Liam nodded slowly as if processing what Julia had said.

"I guess I did come on strong with the whole friend thing," Liam said.

Julia nodded. He had.

"It was more for me than for you. When Dax told me about this stalker . . . it scared me how quickly I had to come out here. I needed to make sure you were okay," Liam said.

"Oh," Julia breathed.

"In my line of work, I don't do relationships. Hell, even friendships are few and far between, but that seemed safer than feeling anything more. The reiteration that we're friends, that was for me. Not for you," Liam said. It sounded as if he was being just as honest as Julia had been.

"Oh," Julia said softly again. She wasn't sure what else to say. Liam was worried he felt too much for Julia? Those words may have been exactly what she would've wanted to hear in years past. But now, Julia knew she deserved more. She deserved a man like Ellis. At least she hoped she did. Because she sure wanted a man like Ellis.

"It may be hard to believe for someone like you who's been surrounded by people who care about you all your life. But in a job like mine? Good friendships are hard to find. I never know who I can really trust. Who truly has my back. But in a weird way, I've always counted on you to have mine, even though the need never arose. And now I'm here to show you I have yours," Liam said.

Julia swallowed. Liam had basically just summed up her years in Hollywood with a few short sentences.

"You'd be surprised how easy it is for me to understand that," Julia said.

"Because you're that great of an actress?" Liam said in a light voice that was a cross between serious and teasing.

"Because it's my life too. And Liam, I think I've always counted on you to be one of my people too," Julia said honestly. Because in a strange way, she had. Even though Liam had been the one who'd gotten away, he'd always come back. At the strangest of times. When she needed him most. Like now.

"So an atypical friendship, it is?" Liam asked, putting his hand out to shake.

Atypical friendship was about the perfect way to sum up their relationship.

"Yes," Julia responded, sealing the deal by claiming Liam's handshake.

CHAPTER EIGHT

PIPER WATCHED as Brock held Kristie next to him on the couch, his arm protectively around her shoulders. It had taken all of a five-minute conversation with Piper for Brock to understand why Kristie had denied his proposal, and he was in her room begging for her forgiveness ten minutes later. The ten minutes had only occurred because Piper had spoken to Brock at his house, and that was the duration of the drive between the two homes. They were now cuter than ever, although Carter still wasn't the couple's biggest fan. He loved each of them individually—well, he loved Kristie and had even come to like Brock —but, as he had explained to Piper, no Daddy liked to see his little girl date.

"So, Dad," Kristie said as she sat on the couch beside Brock, both looking the picture of health. It was hard to imagine that one had just gone into remission from childhood cancer and the other . . . Piper couldn't think about Kristie's diagnosis.

Right after Kristie had been told she was terminal, that there was no more the doctors could feasibly do, Piper had wanted to fight. She'd heard of experimental treatments, other avenues to prolong life. But when she'd brought those options to Kristie's attention, Kristie had cried. It was the first time she'd cried since the initial conversation with the doctors that the cancer had spread too far and fast. That no chemo, radiation, or drugs would be able to save Kristie's perfect little body. Piper had been shocked by Kristie's tears until Kristie begged her mom to stop. To stop trying to save her. Kristie was so tired of all the medication, the constant chemo, the nausea, the hair loss. She was so tired of fighting an unbeatable battle. She wanted to follow the doctors' advice, to live out the rest of her life in peace. She didn't want to keep following the tiny ray of hope that she was sure would eventually amount to nothing. She wanted quality over quantity of life.

Those words had nearly killed Piper. But it wasn't up to Piper. Kristie had already fought so long and hard. It had been enough. Piper had to let her little girl know that everything she'd done was more than enough. But giving in to her dear, sweet girl had been the first part of letting go. And that was still an everyday struggle for Piper. As well as for Carter. They often stayed up after Kristie went to bed, voicing their wishes and concerns. But every night they came to the same conclusion. This was what Kristie wanted. They wanted what Kristie wanted. And they would deal with the consequences on their own. After Kristie . . .

"Earth to dad," Kristie said as she waved a hand in front of Carter's face. He sat on the loveseat next to the couch where Kristie and Brock were cuddled together. Piper was about to chuckle at Carter's zoning out. He tended to do that any time Kristie and Brock got too physically close for his Daddy heart— it was self-preservation. But Piper's urge to laugh flew out the window when she realized Carter was watching her.

"Are you okay?" he mouthed, and she realized he'd noticed her zoning out. She wondered what the look on her face had been as she'd watched Kristie.

"Fine," Piper mouthed back with a smile that felt a little forced. Piper worked hard so that she could feel genuine joy in the little time she still had with Kristie. It was what Kristie needed. But it was hard not to let reality creep in. To think that their time was almost up . . . nope, those thoughts were going to bed for the night.

"Sorry about that, Kristie," Carter said, moving his gaze from Piper to his daughter. The look of concern he'd just given Piper often graced his face when it came to Kristie, but it had been years since that tender side of him had been bestowed on her. And Piper wasn't sure how she felt about that.

"What did you need?" Carter asked, giving Kristie his undivided attention.

"I was just wondering when you're going back to work," she said.

Piper bit her lip. Kristie was crossing the line they'd painted in their family. All talk of after Kristie was gone—tears bit at Piper's eyes, but she kept them at bay—wasn't supposed to happen. At least not in front of Kristie.

It wasn't that Kristie was in denial. She just knew the melancholy those conversations would bring. And since she had no future—emotion welled within Piper's chest—she didn't feel the need to discuss it. Piper didn't either. Her future without Kristie really didn't matter much to her.

"Um . . . I'm not going back," Carter responded, and Piper felt her eyes go wide.

What had Carter said? His job was his life. The reason he'd left Whisling. The reason he'd left them. Piper had always known they'd gotten married too young. But they'd been so in love that nothing had seemed too powerful for them to overcome together. And maybe that would've been the case had they not sided differently on *so* many subjects. Especially when it came to moving from Whisling. Piper had always assumed she would follow Carter to the ends of the earth, but when it had come down to leaving the home they'd created for their daughter who had spent so much of her childhood sick or following Carter's adventures, the first had to matter more. No, that wasn't exactly fair. Carter hadn't wanted to leave just for the adventures. He'd wanted the family to be closer to other medical facilities . . . and he'd wanted adventures. If Piper could've seen those adventures as a way for them to grow together the way Carter had, maybe it would've worked. But Piper had seen the adventures as Carter's way of getting away from the somberness of dealing with a nine-year-old in remission. So she'd told him to go, never actually expecting him to do so. Now, Piper could see that she had pushed Carter as much as he'd pulled away. But six years ago it hadn't felt like that at all.

"You're quitting YouTube?" Kristie asked, her eyes as round as Piper's felt. The shockwaves were still rippling through their home. Even Brock looked surprised.

"No. No, nothing like that. The channel is doing better than ever. Apparently my viewers like watching other people besides me travel. I'll stay on in an administrative role—there's plenty of desk work necessary to keep the channel going—but I don't know. I guess these old bones are in need of a bit of rest. Whisling seems like the right place to make my permanent home," Carter said, shooting Kristie the sweet smile that had first stolen Piper's heart.

But even that smile couldn't take Piper out of her state of shock. What had Carter said? He was settling down? She had assumed that as soon as Kristie . . . as soon as he had nothing tethering him to Whisling, he'd be gone again. But he wasn't going to leave?

"You *are* getting old," Kristie agreed, seeming to understand Carter's decision in a way Piper didn't. But her response earned a raised eyebrow from Carter. Brock scooted away from his girlfriend as Carter stood because they all knew what was coming next.

"Daddy, Daddy," Kristie said, her voice filled with a warning tone that her giggles offset. "I'm too old for this."

Carter ignored Kristie's warnings and began tickling her as she flailed her arms and legs, Brock's reason for moving away. Kristie rolled into a ball, covering her most ticklish spots—her sides—before continuing to try to kick her dad away.

Carter was laughing nearly as hard as Kristie, and Brock and Piper were unable to keep from joining them.

Finally, Kristie landed a kick at Carter's knee, causing him to stumble, and she jumped up in victory before landing back on the couch, completely out of breath.

Piper tried to keep her face the picture of calm as she watched Kristie work to catch her breath. Piper wanted to scream at Carter—he should've taken it easier on their daughter —but she knew that was the last thing Kristie wanted.

Kristie would have these moments of weakness, but she didn't want those she loved to prepare for them. She wanted to be treated the way she'd always been, even if it took her many moments longer to recatch her breath. And even if she had to go to bed at seven some evenings. None of those things were to be dwelt upon. The fact that she was still here—with her hair growing back, as she liked to point out—was what the family was to focus on.

"Are you okay, Carter?" Piper finally asked, trying not to grit her teeth. The not gritting part was made a little easier when it was evident Kristie had completely regained her breath.

"Fine, fine," Carter said. "I should've known all those years of soccer would leave you with a pretty wicked right kick," he teased.

Kristie gave a toothy grin in response. "And don't you forget it," she said, earning a chuckle from her father.

Piper, finally remembering why she'd joined the group in the living room, declared, "Dinner is ready."

She smiled as Carter and Brock quickly scrambled up. Each waited, working hard to refrain from offering a hand of help to Kristie. She didn't want to be babied.

Kristie soon joined them, and they all walked to the dining room where Piper had already set the table. Setting the table used to be a family job, but Kristie had been weakening slowly but surely. Piper had noticed how much it took out of her daughter to do the mundane tasks, especially later in the evening. If Piper had assigned the job to just Carter or Brock, Kristie wouldn't have allowed it. So Piper quietly set the table on her own, hoping Kristie wouldn't take offense.

The quick look of gratitude Kristie shot Piper's way was all she needed to know she'd done the right thing. Piper began dishing up plates as Kristie and Brock sat at the table and Carter helped take plates from the stove to the table.

"This looks delicious, Mom," Kristie said as she sank her head lower to get a better whiff of the spaghetti and tomato sauce on her plate. Their family had always been the meat sauce type until Kristie's stomach couldn't handle the smell of ground meat. It had started during her second round of chemo after her first remission but had been one of the weird things that had stuck, even many months later.

"I'm so glad, Sweetie," Piper said as she kissed the tufts of curls on Kristie's head that gave the appearance of a halo. Kristie's hair had been as straight as Piper's all of her life, even after her first bout with cancer. But for some reason, it had come back curly, more of a typical blonde and less of a strawberry blonde, after this last chemo treatment. Piper loved that the blonde, short curls made Kristie look more like her father.

Piper and Carter sat before Brock offered a blessing on the food, and the family dug in. Piper had to admit, she might not miss the ground beef, but she sure did miss parmesan cheese on her pasta. But that was another strong smell Kristie couldn't abide, so they'd stopped buying it. Along with anything else that made Kristie's stomach roil. It stunk for the family, but it was so much worse for Kristie. Some of her favorite foods, including Swiss cheese and pepperoni, were on that list.

Dinner passed quickly. Kristie ate about half of what Piper had served her before she gave a big yawn.

Carter sent a look in Brock's direction that had him saying he had to get home, and Kristie's sleepy eyes didn't even seem to notice the interaction.

"See you tomorrow," Brock said as he gave Kristie a quick, chaste kiss on the lips, still earning himself a glare from Carter.

"Love you," she said.

"Love you way more," Brock responded before hurrying out of the house. He knew he was pushing his luck with Carter every time he declared his love for the man's daughter in front of him. But Carter's wrath was worth it to Brock. As long as he made Kristie happy.

Kristie slowly pushed herself off her chair. Piper longed to help her but knew she'd be rebuffed, so she stayed seated.

"Love you, guys," Kristie said, dropping a kiss on Piper's cheek when she walked by and then doing the same to Carter.

"Love you to infinity." Carter said the phrase Kristie had used as a child, causing her and Piper to laugh. Piper was grateful for that bit of laughter because, once again, she'd been near tears. Watching her strong girl turn into this frail version of herself was one of the hardest things Piper had ever endured. Sure, the chemo had done worse, but the chemo was hurting Kristie in the name of saving her. Except it hadn't. And now the cancer was finishing its job. Piper *hated* cancer.

"Love you," Piper said as Kristie walked down the short hall to her bedroom.

Piper finally let go of the tears she'd been holding in all day.

Carter, used to this chain of events, walked around the table to hold his ex-wife in his arms before leading her to the couch. He sat Piper down on the couch, handed her the remote, and then headed back into the kitchen to clean up, the way he had for the last couple of months. Although Carter lived in an apartment on Elliot Drive, he spent the majority of his time in Piper and Kristie's home. And he spent that time not just with them but taking care of them. He knew that at this point of the day, Piper had given it her all. She had nothing left. So Carter took over as Piper let mind-numbing reality television fill the screen in front of her. Anything to keep her thoughts off her future and the bleakness life would have when the glue that held their little family together was no longer on this earth.

CHAPTER NINE

"CHOCOLATE FOR BREAKFAST, and then it's time to get off the couch," Nora said to Amber and Elise as they joined her in the kitchen.

Nora's one-bedroom was pretty tiny, so she'd given her bed, after much persuasion, to the girls to share. She was out in the living room on the pull-out couch.

Nora had decorated the small but cozy apartment in blues and greens, and the peaceful colors somehow made the space seem larger.

After the news they'd received in the diner that their boss wasn't going to sell them the company they'd assumed would be theirs, the girls had wallowed for two days. Nora had given them that time to mourn the loss of what they'd thought their future was going to be, but now it was time to move. Maybe not move on, but at least move. Literally. She had a hiked planned for them that morning after they finished their chocolate chip pancakes.

"Chocolate. Good move, Mama Nora," Elise said as she sleepily slid into one of the empty chairs at Nora's island that doubled as her dining table.

Nora piled their two plates high with stacks of her world-famous chocolate chip pancakes. Maybe *world-famous* was a stretch, but her nieces and nephew sure seemed to like them.

She handed Elise the butter dish and Amber the bottle of syrup and let the girls dress their pancakes the way they preferred.

Amber shot Nora a smile of gratitude as she took the butter dish from her sister. Nora thought Amber was probably just as disappointed as Elise, but she didn't seem to be taking the news as hard. At least not outwardly. But if Amber was anything like Nora, it was hitting her just as painfully. She was just good at hiding her true feelings. Nora wondered if she'd inherited that trait or if Amber really was doing okay. Nora hoped the latter because she doubted Amber would want to talk about her feelings, no matter how sad she was, when it was apparent Elise was hurting so much right next to her.

After each had downed nearly their entire plate of pancakes, Nora decided it was time for the second thing on her list that would get them out of their sad funk.

"As soon as you two are finished, we're going on a hike," she announced.

Amber pursed her lips in thought but gave way to an amused expression as soon as she registered the look of shock on Elise's face.

"Did you say *a hike?*" Elise asked, her mouth still full of half-chewed pancake. "Like when we go outdoors and walk outdoors and hike—"

"Outdoors," Nora finished for her. "I think it would be good for us."

"Good for us?" Elise's voice squeaked on the last word, and Amber nearly lost her battle of trying to keep a straight face as a single grunt of a laugh escaped.

"Do you think this is a good idea?" Elise turned to Amber

whose lips kept quirking in an attempt to keep her humor within.

Amber shrugged as she finally just bit down on her lip to keep from laughing and then drew in a deep breath before saying, "I don't think it's any worse of an idea than anything we've done the past couple of days."

Elise leaned back in her dining stool thoughtfully, finally finishing chewing the bite of food in her mouth. "I guess not," she said quietly. "And I imagine the views on this hike will be pretty magnificent?"

"We *are* on Whisling," Nora said in lieu of an answer.

Elise nodded. "Okay, fine. But if I keel over at any point during this hike, it's up to one of you to find a devastatingly good-looking man to come and rescue me. Mack would work if he weren't already in love with Mama Nora. I need a man who will fall in love with *me*. Got it?"

Elise looked from Amber to Nora, who had a slight blush to her cheeks at the mention of Mack being in love with her. Mack was her friend. Her good friend. But in love with her? Pshaw.

"If you keel over, I'll find you two good-looking men," Nora promised as a way to distract everyone from her blush.

Elise nodded with a smile. "A love triangle. I like the way you think, Mama Nora," she said as she stood and went toward the bedroom to change out of her pajamas.

She turned her head back just as she reached the bedroom door. "Thank you. I think you're right. This is exactly what we need."

Elise disappeared into the room, and Nora knew she had just a few moments alone with Amber.

"How are you? Really," Nora quietly asked Amber, who sat watching the doorway her sister had gone through.

Amber shrugged once again. She'd been doing that quite a bit lately.

"I'll be fine. It's the death of a dream, so it hurts. But the end of one thing just means the beginning of another, right?" Amber asked, a little too optimistically.

"It's okay to be sad," Nora said.

"Oh, I am sad," Amber replied with a small smile. "I'm not really a wallower, though. That's more Elise. I'm a 'jump back on the horse and figure out a way to ride out of town' kind of girl."

Nora chuckled since Amber was still smiling. "I like the analogy."

"Thanks. It just came to me in the moment," Amber said proudly.

Nora smiled. It really did seem as if Amber was okay.

Elise came back into the room a few moments later wearing yoga pants, a workout tank, and a pair of running shoes.

"I'm as ready as I'll ever be," Elise said, causing Amber to look from Nora, who'd already dressed in the same type of gear earlier, back to Elise.

"I'd better get ready as well. I'll be back out in a jiff," Amber said, jumping up to run to the bedroom as Elise scurried to the bathroom to brush her teeth.

The three were out the door and piled into Nora's car a few moments later, and she took off for the place she'd decided to take the girls. It was more of an inclined walk than a true hike, but Nora figured it was better to prepare the two for the worst.

The car ride was full of music and quiet pondering, except for the few times Elise's jams played and she sang along at the top of her lungs. After a thirty-minute drive, Nora pulled off to the side of the road on the east side of the island. It was definitely less traveled than downtown, but there were still a couple of other cars parked there already. The beautiful lush trees and greenery that were native to Washington would surround them the minute they got out of the car and into the dense vegetation.

"This is gorgeous," Elise breathed as she tugged the coat she'd thrown on over her workout gear a little closer. It was a pretty mild November morning, but between the humidity and the slight breeze, there was quite a chill in the air. Nora was glad she'd brought her heavier coat as well.

The women got out of the car and started walking along the path that had been forged through the woods many years before.

"Do you ever wonder who created the trails we walk?" Amber asked as the other two women nodded.

"I was actually just wondering the same thing," Nora said as she continued to concentrate on not tripping over the many roots lying along the pathway.

"How long ago it was made? What their purpose was?" Elise added.

The women fell back into their own thoughts as they took the trail slowly. It really wasn't a grueling hike, but they were beginning to go uphill. And after not working out for a while, the trail was starting to take its toll.

All three of them were breathing deeply, as Nora liked to put it. Although the panting that accompanied their breathing indicated that they weren't breathing deeply as much as trying very hard to catch their breath.

Elise stopped them at a large tree that she "had to examine," and the other two women were more than ready for the break also. Nora handed out the water bottles she'd packed in her bag, and the other two gratefully accepted as Amber leaned against a tree opposite from the one Elise was inspecting.

"I think this is a Western Hemlock," Elise said as she took in the size and shape of the tree that Nora thought looked like a gigantic Christmas tree. She may have been the resident of the island, but it didn't mean she knew much about the botany. Sure, it was all pretty to look at, but Nora was a bit ashamed to admit she knew nothing about the names or types of trees they were walking through.

Elise looked to Nora for confirmation on her claim.

"Sure?" she said with a shrug, and Elise laughed before smiling up at the sun. "Should we get moving again?" she asked, and the other two nodded as Nora gathered the water bottles.

Nora had taken this trail a couple times before but had never gone this far in. They'd passed a few other groups during their first hour on the trail, but for that last half hour or so, they seemed to be all alone. Nora wondered how far they'd traveled and if it was about time to turn around and head back to the car.

She voiced her question.

"The path still seems pretty well traveled. How about we turn around in half an hour or when the path seems to get a little hazy?" Elise asked, and Amber nodded quickly in agreement.

Nora was glad her plan had worked. Both girls seemed much happier than they'd been before, even on the car ride over, but she knew her legs would be aching the next day. She figured it was worth it.

Amber took the lead this time, and the three women walked along the trail, the sounds of twittering birds sometimes all they could hear. As they continued to walk, Nora began to hear a sound she thought they'd left behind on Elliot drive.

Nora swore she heard the sound of waves breaking on the shore.

"Do you hear that?" Elise asked a few seconds after Nora had first heard the sounds of the ocean.

"Water, right?" Amber asked, and Elise nodded, both of them picking up their pace.

Nora had to agree she was pretty curious as well. The distance between the trees seemed to be growing, and there was more sunlight on their path.

Suddenly, Amber stopped with a gasp. Elise moved around her and stopped short as well. Nora got on her tiptoes and craned her neck to see between their shoulders. In front of them was a wide expanse of overgrown brush. Nora imagined it had been completely cleared once upon a time, but it had been neglected over the years. Beyond the clearing was a gigantic wooden home. The kind you expected to see in the western mountains, not on Whisling. But Nora doubted either of those things was what had stopped the girls in their tracks. Her eyes moved to the right side of the clearing, to a sea cliff that dropped right into the beautiful, gray Pacific.

"Our very own Cliffs of Moher," Elise breathed as the other women just stood in awe. The view was truly a thing of beauty.

Amber finally walked a bit further so that she was in the clearing, and that let Elise loose. She ran toward the house, and Amber quickly followed.

Nora walked behind them at a sedate pace, taking in all that was around her. She'd had no idea this was up here. Why wasn't it talked about more? Judging by the look of the home, it was no longer lived in. Was that why people kept it a secret? To protect the vacant home?

"It's like a dream," Elise yelled back to Amber and Nora as she took the steps up to the wraparound front porch.

"Watch your step!" Nora called out, worried about rotting wood.

"It's not as neglected as you'd think," Elise responded before carefully walking her way around the front porch and peering into the windows. "Yup, not a single piece of furniture. Why is this place abandoned?" she asked as Amber joined her.

"The front room is so big," Amber said loudly enough for Nora to hear.

"Oh my gosh. Look at this kitchen," Elise squealed, and Nora smiled as Elise raced around to the back of the house.

A sudden piercing shriek met Nora and Amber's ears, and assuming the worst, they raced around the house to see a very unhurt but excited Elise pointing to the backyard.

"It has a barn. A gigantic, beautiful barn. The kind people would kill to have events in," she said slowly as if a thought was taking shape.

"Um nope. Nope, nope, nope. I know that face," Amber said.

Elise held up a hand. "Before you say nope–" she started.

"Already said nope. Many times," Amber replied.

"Just hear me out," Elise said.

"Fine." Amber crossed her arms across her chest.

"Really hear me," Elise pleaded, and Amber dropped her arms.

"We were about to buy an event company," Elise said.

Amber nodded. "Yes, one of the most sought after companies in Kansas City," she replied.

"True," Elise said quietly before adding, "But one that had been built from the ground up."

"Thirty years ago," Amber countered.

"In a highly competitive arena," Elise said before turning to Nora.

"How many event companies are on the island?" Elise asked.

"Oh, um, as far as I know, none. But the country club has someone to oversee events there," Nora said as both Elise and Amber stared at her, their expressions unreadable.

"None, Amber. No competition. We were always fighting for top spot in KC," Elise said.

Amber crossed her arms again. "Elise. This is a tiny island. I can guarantee there are dozens if not hundreds of event companies in Seattle. Just a ferry ride away."

"A ferry ride away. You said it, Amber. There is no one here. On site. Who knows the ins and outs of local commerce and culture. Mama Nora said so."

"I said *as far as I know . . .*" Nora let her voice trail off because it was evident no one was listening to her anyway.

"This location is gorgeous. Like breathtakingly stunning," Elise said as she turned in a circle, her arms outstretched.

"It is," Amber conceded. "But the buildings are run down."

"They're in decent shape for being vacant," Elise countered.

"From what we can tell standing outside," Amber clarified.

Elise pursed her lips.

"Let's try. Please, Amber? When one door closes, a window opens. What if this is our window? We can't close our window, Ams," Elise nearly begged.

Amber looked from the barn to the house and then at the ocean view, her eyes lingering there.

"How would we even get guests back here? We can't ask them to hike for two hours."

"There has to be a trail for vehicles if this house is back here," Elise replied.

"What about Mom and Dad? Can we really leave Kansas City for good?" Amber asked softly.

Elise met her eyes. "I think they'd understand. Without KC Weddings, I don't think I'd stay in Missouri anyway. Would you?" she asked.

Amber paused before slowly shaking her head. "I couldn't go work for any of our competitors, but I don't think I could stay and work for Rochelle's family either"

"Exactly," Elise said. "Besides, here we'd have family."

Elise waved a hand toward Nora, who was trying not to get her hopes up. Elise and Amber living here on Whisling? This was better than a dream come true for her. But she would only be happy if this was really their best option.

"That's true. And Mom and Dad would fall in love with this view," Amber said.

"Everyone would fall in love with this view. I know there

will be roadblocks and hurdles—I'm not a complete nincompoop —but the pay off? Amber, this place. Don't you feel it?"

Amber paused, still looking toward the sea cliff. "I do," she murmured, and that was enough for Elise.

"I promise you, if it gets to be too much, I'll walk away," Elise said as she practically jumped on Amber to hug her.

Amber returned the hug with a smile. "I have a feeling our definitions of *too much* will be quite different," she said from within her sister's embrace.

"Let's cross that bridge when we get there, shall we?" Elise said with a gigantic, goofy grin, causing Amber and Nora to laugh.

Nora had a feeling these girls were in for the ride of their lives.

CHAPTER TEN

ALEXIS TURNED this way and that in front of her full-length mirror, taking all of herself in from her long black hair to her camel-colored booties. She doubted that Peter or Brittany cared about how she looked, but she wanted to appear perfect nonetheless. There was very little she had control over with this afternoon date. But her appearance was all up to her, so it would be perfect. And then maybe this formal introduction could go perfectly as well? Alexis would continue wishing.

When Alexis had spoken to Jared about what Lou's youngest, Hazel, had told them, Jared had been appalled, then sorrowful, then somewhat resolved. He immediately realized talking to Marsha wouldn't help his case—the woman had a vendetta against Alexis and Margie and, honestly, even Alexis couldn't fully fault Marsha for that. Sure, most mature adults would've been able to see that Alexis and Margie could join Marsha's circle instead of being treated as interlopers. But when Alexis tried really hard to see Marsha's point of view, she could see it. The woman who was taking her dad away had a daughter who was now dating her ex-husband. Alexis couldn't let her mind dwell on the fact that Marsha had cheated on said husband, and even after he'd tried to work it out, she'd still walked away from their marriage. But she could see how in Marsha's twisted reality, Alexis and Margie were stealing those she loved. Fine.

So talking to Marsha seemed out of the question. At least for now. Alexis hadn't promised anything to Jared because, if times got desperate, who knew what Alexis would do.

Jared then began to take the burden solely upon himself, saying if he'd just introduced Alexis to the kids earlier, none of this would've been a problem. If they'd seen how amazing she was, they wouldn't have been able to agree with their mom.

Alexis didn't agree that any of the situation was Jared's fault, nor did she think that if his kids had already known her, none of this would've happened. But she did agree that it was time to meet Jared's kids. To let them know she was on their side. By their side.

So the date had been set. And it was here. Today. Alexis thought of all the things she'd rather be doing. Getting a cavity filled with no Novocaine, jumping out of an airplane regardless of her intense fear of heights. She knew what this meeting meant. If she met Jared's kids and they still hated her? What could he do? He couldn't pick Alexis. He was the best kind of dad there was. He would choose his kids. The way Alexis would want him to. But where would that leave them? Alexis couldn't think about it. She just had to get those kids to love her. There was no alternative.

A knock sounded on her front door, and Alexis hurried to open it before Margie could. Alexis wasn't sure what Marsha had told her kids about Margie—probably something about how she was stealing their grandpa away—so the less reminder they had that Margie and Alexis were family, the better.

"Hey." Alexis breathed a bit easier when she saw a very handsome Jared at her front door. He'd left his caramel brown hair messy, just the way Alexis liked it. He wore a Henley and dark jeans, the picture of a perfect boyfriend. But as badly as Alexis wanted to lean in and let him know how much she appreciated the look, she didn't. Because out of the corner of her gaze, she could see four very intent eyes taking in her every move.

She felt her entire body go stiff.

"It'll be fine," Jared assured as he took her hand without going in for their typical predate kiss.

Alexis realized he also understood that a kiss wouldn't be the smartest move in front of his kids.

Those four eyes went straight to their joined hands, and Alexis pulled hers away quickly. She didn't want to press her luck.

As they got closer to the car, Brittany scooted back in her seat as if she hadn't just been leaning over her brother to get a better look at Alexis. The scowls on both their faces didn't bode well for Alexis. But she could turn that around. She had to.

Alexis felt the pace they were taking to get to the car was a bit too slow, so she didn't wait for Jared to open her door and quickly joined the children in the car.

"Hi, Brittany, Peter," she said cheerfully, turning around to greet both children. Scowls were the only things Alexis got in response.

"See, I told you," Brittany said without acknowledging Alexis at all. "Daddy loves Mom way more. He didn't even open the door for this one."

Alexis felt her bright smile dim a bit, but she couldn't let Brittany's words get to her. Even if the young girl had tried to be as cruel as she could.

Jared opened his car door, thankfully missing that whole exchange, and sat down before turning around to look at his kids.

"Peter, Brittany, did you say *hello*?" Jared asked.

Neither made a move to say anything, so Alexis tried to jump to their defense. Maybe if she immediately took their side, they would begin to thaw toward her.

"We were just getting acquainted," Alexis said, shooting her smile at Jared and then at his kids.

Still scowling.

Well, they were just a few minutes in. What did Alexis expect?

"Peter thought it would be fun to go to the arcade," Jared said, turning to look back at his son who gave a brief nod.

"And then Brittany loves going shopping at the boutiques on Elliot. Maybe we could do that after?" Jared asked, glancing at his daughter.

"I like shopping there with *Mom*. Or with you," Brittany said pointedly.

"And now it could be fun to go with Alexis too." Jared was trying so hard, and Alexis loved him all the more for it.

"Doubt it," Brittany muttered, but the car had started, so Alexis was pretty sure Jared hadn't heard what she'd said.

Thank goodness.

Jared drove their little group down to the pier where there were a few carnival games, some small amusement rides, and then a large arcade—the main draw for their group, apparently.

"So you're in seventh grade?" Alexis asked, turning to look at Peter.

"*He's* in seventh grade," Brittany said with all the annoyance a preteen could muster.

"Yup," Alexis said brightly. "I was speaking to Peter."

"Ri-ight," Brittany said, and Alexis's stomach turned. This was not going well. Brittany wasn't just saying mean things. She was actively trying to make Alexis look bad, as if she couldn't keep Jared's kids straight. Not that Jared would care about that, but still. This felt like a step in the wrong direction.

"Do you like middle school, Peter?" Alexis used his name so no one could accuse her of anything more.

"I guess," Peter said.

Okay, that line of questioning was going nowhere. Sports. Boys loved sports, right? She was sure Jared had told her about Peter playing competitive soccer.

"Are you playing any sports right now?" Alexis asked, and Brittany burst out laughing.

"Like the gimp could play any sports," Brittany said as she pointed down to the floor of the car where, sure enough, a brace covered Peter's foot. Oh good heavens.

"Brittany!" Jared reprimanded as he slammed on the brakes at a red light.

"Sorry," Brittany muttered as Jared turned to Alexis.

"Peter sprained his foot a couple days ago. I haven't had a chance to tell you. But it's totally not a big deal." Jared said the last words loudly for the sake of Brittany, but Alexis still felt mortified.

She totally understood Jared not telling her about the injury. She and Jared hadn't done anything other than text the fact that they were alive to one another these past few days because things were crazy with both their jobs, with Jared's family and with Alexis's mom's wedding. They had barely been able to set up this one date. She didn't blame Jared for not passing on the news.

As Alexis glanced back, she saw that Peter's scowl was gone. It was now replaced by puppy dog eyes full of sorrow. Crud!

Alexis fought the urge to drop her head into her hands. This couldn't get any worse, could it?

Alexis decided questions should maybe be saved until she could see the entirety of the children's bodies.

"Brittany, do you want to tell Alexis about the play you'll be in?" Jared asked as they drove down Elliot Drive, thankfully only a few blocks from the pier. Things had to get better once arcade games were involved.

"Nope," Brittany popped. When she saw her father glaring in the rearview mirror, with arms crossed over her chest, in a monotone voice she said, "I'm in a play."

"What part are you playing?" Alexis couldn't stay silent now that Brittany had said something.

"The evil stepsister," Brittany replied, and Alexis swore the little girl put her emphasis on evil, causing a chill to run down Alexis's spine.

Jared finally pulled into a parking spot and both kids threw open their doors, saving Alexis from having to respond. Brittany jumped out of the car, and Peter got out a little more slowly.

Jared ran around to open Alexis's car door, but she couldn't let him do that. Not when he had a kid with a sprained foot. So Alexis pointed to Peter and Jared nodded, understanding where Alexis wanted him to put his priority.

Brittany went around to the back of the car, getting a pair of crutches from the trunk and then moving around to the side of the car to hand them off to her dad.

Alexis joined them just in time to hear Brittany say, "Look. The whole *family* is helping Peter."

And then she shot Alexis a glare that told her where she stood in Brittany's book.

Jared missed the look, since Brittany was behind him while he helped Peter, and he shot Alexis a happy smile. He must've thought the *family* comment was a good thing. Poor man. If he only knew. Alexis would've laughed if she didn't feel like her world was unraveling with every figurative pull of Brittany's figurative fingers.

No. She couldn't start to think of Brittany as the enemy. She couldn't even think of Marsha as the enemy. They were family, so if Alexis wanted to be a part of one of their lives, it was all or nothing. She had to shoot for loving them all.

They moved slowly down the pier and toward the arcade where both kids immediately held out their hands for money. Once it was received, they were gone.

Alexis wouldn't dwell on how spoiled that gesture seemed and instead breathed a sigh of relief at getting a small reprieve. She had to regroup. She wasn't going into battle against Brittany. But how did she prove that to her?

"Brittany is a bit much. She's been going through a hard time since the divorce. It might be hard for you to imagine, but she used to be the sweetest little girl. There wasn't a sassy bone in that body."

At first, that was difficult to imagine. But Alexis tried to envision that cute, little girl. It wasn't too hard considering Brittany was still in the fifth grade, that age when a child could look older and then younger, all within moments of each other. Alexis could visualize Brittany as a five-year-old with little, blonde pigtails and defined freckles on her cute, little nose. Maybe the image of that sweetheart would help her when Brittany came back?

"And Peter's been a grouch since he sprained his foot at his soccer game. But he'll come around soon," Jared promised as he put an arm around Alexis's shoulders. She sighed as she leaned into his strength. This was why she was doing this. Jared was worth it. Their relationship was worth it. And she had a feeling once she got to know his kids, really know them, they'd be worth it too. It was just getting to know them that might be the issue.

What seemed like moments later, the kids came back, both out of money. But when Alexis looked down at her watch, she saw that an entire hour had passed. How did time fly like that when she was with Jared? Peter immediately let his dad know that he needed the restroom, and because Jared didn't want him to do the trek on crutches alone, he whispered, "Will you be okay if I leave you with Brit?"

"Of course," Alexis said with a smile. She felt ready to take on the world again now that she'd spent nearly an hour curled up against Jared's side.

Brittany kicked at a small rock along the wooden pier as her brother and dad left. She followed the rock until she kicked it over the side and then laid her chin against the tall railing overlooking the ocean, reminding Alexis how small she truly was. The poor girl was just fighting for what she felt was hers. Her family. Alexis had to admire that.

Alexis decided to take the spot on the rail next to her, her chest hitting the railing. Alexis lifted her arms so that she could lean them against the rail.

"Evil stepsister, huh?" Alexis asked, and Brittany didn't acknowledge her.

They watched as the waves rolled in for a few minutes before Brittany said, "You don't have to pretend that you want to get to know me. You can steal my dad without me liking you. It's not like you'll stay around very long anyway."

Alexis swallowed. How did such a little girl know how to say such spiteful things? Alexis knew. She could practically hear those exact same words coming from the girl's mother. But if Alexis was in this for the long haul, she was going to have to deal with Marsha's influence everywhere she looked. And she cared enough about Jared to do it.

"I'm not pretending. I'd like to get to know you. Not just because I like your dad, but because I'm willing to bet you're a pretty cool kid," Alexis said as the wind hit her face, the splash from the waves under them sometimes joining. She was grateful her makeup look was very minimal.

"Oh, yeah? Why would you bet that?" Brittany asked,

turning so that her shoulder was now pressed against the wooden wall under the rail.

"Because your dad has told me a few things. And because you have a cool dad. Some of that had to have rubbed off on you," Alexis said.

"But you hate my mom," Brittany said matter-of-factly.

"I hardly know your mom."

Brittany scoffed.

"Your mom is marrying Grandpa, and you want to steal my dad. You should know my mom," Brittany said, and Alexis realized that was true. Not the stealing part but the rest of it.

"You're right."

Brittany's mouth dropped open for a second before she remembered who she was talking to, and she turned to the ocean once again.

"I'm going to bet Daddy will ask you where you want to eat lunch," Brittany said as she looked at the water again. "I don't care where you choose, but can we just not go to Winders? I hate that place," Brittany said.

Alexis nodded. "Of course. We can go anywhere you'd like—" she started, but she was cut off when Brittany turned and ran toward where her father and brother were now walking toward them.

Well, at least Brittany had given her something.

"Shopping or lunch first?" Jared asked.

"Lunch," his children declared in unison.

"Got it. Since you guys chose that, let's let Alexis choose where she wants to go," Jared said.

Peter reluctantly nodded, but Brittany shot Alexis a look that could've only said *I told you so.*

Alexis had been preparing for this moment. Maybe she didn't know where she wanted to go, but she sure could voice where she didn't want to go.

"Anywhere but Winders," Alexis said, shooting a smile at Brittany. "I hate that place." She copied what the girl had said word for word, showing solidarity.

"Oh," Jared said, his face revealing how uncomfortable he felt before he covered it with a painful looking smile.

"That's awkward," Peter added before Jared replied, "No, it's not. It's fine. Totally fine." Jared shot Alexis a smile. What had she done?

"It is awkward, Dad. It's our entire family's favorite restaurant, Uncle Willy owns it, and *Alexis* hates it." Brittany lingered on her name, and Alexis finally realized what had happened. She'd been set up. Big time.

"I don't hate it," Alexis tried to backtrack.

"But you just said you did," Peter pointed out.

"I know. It's just . . ." Should she rat Brittany out? The smile on the girl's face said she was waiting for it. It felt like another trap.

How was this eleven-year-old outsmarting her?

"My foot is kind of getting sore," Peter said after Brittany directed a look his way.

And now she was orchestrating the next part of her plan. Oh, this girl was good. But then Alexis remembered the words Brittany had spoken. How they hadn't sounded like a little girl but rather a grown woman. Like Marsha. Had this all been her? Alexis wouldn't put it past her. But she was supposed to not be seeing her as the enemy. How could she not after all of this?

"We hardly got any time with Alexis," Jared said, but Peter leaned heavily against the wall behind him as if he could no longer stand.

"Dad, it's hurting," he said.

Jared nodded. What else could he do?

"I think we had enough time with Alexis anyway. We know

she likes to tease gimps, and she hates what we like," Brittany said.

Jared glared at his daughter.

"What?" she asked with a raise of her hands.

This had gone worse than Alexis could've imagined. She'd had no idea how deep the children's dislike for her went. Now their time together had come to an end. And Alexis had done nothing to win either child over.

"What about shopping? We could take Peter home and then bring you shopping?"

"I want to go shopping with Mom," Brittany said.

"You could go with her too, but let's all go together now," Jared pleaded.

"I don't want to." Brittany crossed her arms across her chest, and Alexis knew she wasn't budging. Jared seemed to understand that too.

"Fine," he said as he took Alexis's hand. And although their joined hands received glares from both children, Alexis wouldn't let go. Not now. She realized that because Jared's children refused to accept her, her relationship with Jared now had an expiration date. So Alexis was going to hold on for as long as she could. She wasn't ready to give up and let go.

CHAPTER ELEVEN

"HEY, MOM," Kristie said as she poked her head through the door of the master bedroom. Master bedroom was a bit of a stretch for the room Piper resided in, but she guessed since she was technically the master of the home and she resided in the room, it could be called such. Even if there was no en suite and the closet was postage-stamp tiny. But then again, it wasn't like Piper collected clothes or anything, so it worked. That's what she could say about most of her home. It worked . . . and it was theirs. So it was special. At least to them.

"What's up?" Piper asked as she sifted through her closet, looking for something to wear. She needed to go into their tiny attic to pull down her bin of winter clothes, but it was something she avoided every year. Maybe because it had always been Carter's job when he'd lived with them. She knew she could ask Carter to do it for her now, but it didn't seem right when he didn't live with them. It almost felt like too intimate a task. Was that strange? Although everything in Piper's life felt pretty strange at the moment.

"I just . . ."

Piper looked up when she heard the hesitation in Kristie's

voice, and then she noticed the concern in Kristie's big, green eyes.

Piper moved from her task at the closet and sat on the zebra comforter on her bed behind her. It was a purchase she'd made to try to celebrate her freedom from Carter. A purchase that she now kind of regretted. Okay, she definitely regretted it.

Kristie walked into the room and took the seat her mom offered, sinking into the bed as soon as she sat. The plush mattress was another thing Piper would've liked to replace in her home if she could. Her back, which was growing older by the moment, would love a firmer mattress to sleep on. But those kinds of purchases were out of reach. The ever-mounting medical bills would never allow for buying non-necessities.

"Would you ever get back together with Dad?" Kristie asked suddenly.

Piper tried not to rear back in shock, without success. What the what?

"I know you and Dad got divorced for good reason. I get that. But now that he's back . . . he's going to stay here, Mom. Wasn't that the main reason you guys separated?" Kristie asked.

Piper had known her daughter was astute, but this was almost too much. Piper had never told her daughter the reasons for their divorce, only that it was what was best for all of them and they both still loved her, so nothing else mattered.

But of course Kristie had dug past the excuses Piper had given and gone straight to the core of the issue. The way she always did. Her girl was fearless.

"It was. The main catalyst. But honestly, I think if we were really meant to be together, we would've worked through that," Piper said, trying to be as frank with Kristie as she could.

When Kristie had been told by the doctors there was nothing more they could do to fight her cancer, she had asked two things of her parents. That they always be honest with her and that the three of them work on living in the present. Because the future wasn't promised to Kristie, or any of them for that matter. Piper had made that promise and worked hard to fulfill her side of it every day. Even if some days it nearly broke her.

"What if you weren't meant to be together then but you are now?" Kristie asked as she leaned her head on Piper's shoulder.

Piper began to stroke Kristie's short curls, breathing in every moment of this closeness. Something cracked inside of her as she thought about how much she was going to miss this. She knew the memories would pale in comparison to living in these moments, and yet Piper tried to catalogue them. Like her mind was a computer and she'd be able to recall this file when the pain grew to be too much.

Nope, those were future thoughts. Here and now. Here and now Kristie was wondering why her parents weren't together. Okay, Piper could do this.

"Kristie, where is this coming from?" Piper asked as Kristie's head dropped from her shoulder to her lap.

"I'm scared, Mom," Kristie said, and it was easy to hear the raw fear behind those words.

"Oh, sweetie," Piper said, fighting back the tears. They were selfish tears, and right now it was time to focus on Kristie.

"Not for me," Kristie clarified, and the confusion those words caused stopped the tears. Thank goodness.

"I know I'm going to Heaven. Not to toot my own horn, but for a teen, I'm a pretty decent person. I believe in God and that He loves me. I know where I'm going, and I know one day you'll join me. But I have a feeling those days apart will be more lonely for you than they'll be for me. Because I get to go spend time with God. Who am I leaving you with?" Kristie asked.

This time the tears couldn't be stopped. Kristie was breaking her own rule. They were talking about the future, so

Piper figured she could be forgiven for breaking the rule of crying in front of her daughter. Something she'd tried to avoid at all costs. But these were a mix of tears. She was oh so happy that this was her daughter's view of death. This was what she'd hoped Kristie would believe, but how much easier was it to believe when your fate wasn't staring you right in the eye. Kristie was meeting her fate and embracing it. Her fearless girl. But the other part of her tears was that *she* was the cause of any concern for her girl. The girl who could look death in the eye but couldn't bear the thought of leaving her mother alone.

"I'll be fine," Piper began, and then she realized that was a lie. She'd promised to be honest. Even when it was hard.

"Kristie, you're right. When you leave this earth and we are temporarily separated," Piper also believed in an afterlife where she would see Kristie again, "it will leave an unfillable hole in my heart. You are my life and my joy. But I will manage. I will mourn, and then I will live."

"How, Mom?" Kristie asked the question her mother didn't dare to.

"I'm not sure." Piper hated that she had to be honest. She wanted to quell Kristie's fears, but this was one place where Piper didn't have any answers.

"Dad is going to have that same hole, Mom," Kristie said as she sat up again in order to look Piper in the eye.

Piper nodded. If anyone would understand her pain, it would be Carter. They may not have always seen eye to eye on how to best care for Kristie, but one thing was certain, they both loved her completely.

"But if you were there for him and he was there for you . . . I know you still love him," Kristie said.

Piper nodded again. If only love was their issue. But it never had been. Sometimes Piper wondered if she'd loved Carter too much. If that love had felt like a noose for him instead of an embrace.

"I've never stopped loving your father," Piper said honestly.

"He said the same about you," Kristie said.

Piper froze. *He what?*

"Yes, I talked to him," Kristie said, answering Piper's unspoken question. "After that conversation we had when he said he's planning on living here, I was worried about him. So I asked. And he said that's why he's retiring. He wants to be near you after I die."

Piper had never heard Kristie say those last three words aloud, and man, if she didn't hate them even more now. Her eyes misted once again, and she fought hard to not fall victim to the sobs that threatened.

"Mom. Stay with me, Mom." Kristie waved a hand in front of Piper's face, knowing she'd lost her.

"That's something me and your dad will need to talk about, Kristie," Piper croaked, unable to take this all in at once. Too much emotion. Too much pain.

"Dad says he wants to be here, Mom. I know you're worried we kept him back from his dreams," Kristie said as Piper interrupted, "*I* kept him back, Sweetheart. There was no *we* in that."

"Fine, you kept him back. But he said he has new dreams now. To stay here with me for as long as I have and then to be here with you. He realized when he was traveling the world that it was cool and all. And it fulfilled the part of him that he thought needed filling. But when that was filled, he still felt empty. Because he missed us. He needed us."

Piper didn't doubt for a second that Carter had missed them. And he needed Kristie, there was no mistake about that. But the rest of it? She wasn't sure what to think.

"Just say you'll try, Mom." Kristie turned so that she was

facing Piper, her legs crossed on the bed. "I need you to say you'll try. Please, Mom?" Kristie asked.

Piper couldn't say no. Her fearless girl had one fear. And if Piper could dispel it, she would. Even if she wasn't sure how it could ever work out. Because Carter's wanderlust was bound to return, and Piper knew she would never leave Whisling. She could never leave the last place Kristie had called home. It was where they would bury their baby girl, and she couldn't leave her body behind. Even if Kristie's spirit had. Piper would live out her life, however long she had, and then be buried right next to her baby girl. It was all she had left to aspire to. Gone were her dreams of family, career, and any happy future. It would all be lost until she found her Kristie again.

But if Kristie wanted Piper to talk to Carter, she would. She was sure Carter would want to do the same for Kristie's sake. But Piper truly doubted anything would come of that talk. If she knew Carter, he'd want to escape the island and its memories as soon as he could. He was a wanderer. Piper wasn't.

However, even if Piper was bound to fail, she would try. And maybe try again, if that's what Kristie wanted. Because there was nothing out of bounds when it came to giving Kristie what she could. For her daughter, she would do anything. She would give anything. Including talking to her ex about getting back together.

CHAPTER TWELVE

"THERE'S A ROAD. There is a road, people," Elise declared loudly as she flopped back onto the couch in Nora's apartment with a triumphant raise of her arms. She'd gone into the bedroom a few moments before to take a call from the realtor helping them to secure the property on the sea cliffs.

They were seeing this through.

The girls had gone home to Kansas City for Thanksgiving, knowing they had to give the news that they were moving in person. All, including their mother, Tabby, had taken the news relatively well. The fact that they'd led the conversation with the devastating news about losing KC Weddings made everyone more compassionate. Nora was sure the girls' parents were just glad to see they had some direction after being dealt such a blow.

Then they'd come back to Nora's the Monday after the holiday. And now they were working their tails off to secure the property and, more importantly, investors. Although the girls had saved up a good amount, especially for their young ages, and they were soon going to sell their condo for even more cash, they didn't have enough to buy the property on the cliffs as well as the extra capital needed to fix it up. But the news of a road was huge. The cost of putting in a road would've been astronomical.

"It's basically just a dirt path that's wide enough for two cars —just one in some places—but it's enough for now," Elise declared. "Even though parts of the property were neglected, the family did keep up the road so that they could get in and out easily."

Elise's smile was enormous, and Amber's nearly matched Elise's at the news. Things were really moving forward.

Nora felt like now was a great time to add her news as well.

"So, I've been speaking with my financial advisor," she said. The girls nodded politely, but Nora was sure they were wondering why she was bringing this up now. They just had to wait a few more seconds and all would be clear.

"We've consolidated a few of my assets because I'd like to invest," Nora said.

Both girls sat on the couch with blank looks on their faces.

"In you two. In Whisling Island Events," Nora said.

The same look of horror quickly shadowed both beautiful faces.

"No. I'm sorry, but no," Amber said, while Elise just muttered, "No, no, no, no, no."

"Would you mind outlining your concerns with me?" Nora asked, trying to sound as professional as possible. She didn't want the girls to know her feelings had been hurt.

"One, you're my mom," Amber said, and Elise nodded.

"Two, you're a relative," Elise said, and this time Amber nodded.

"So who better to believe in you girls?" Nora asked as she pushed over the papers she'd drawn up with her financial adviser. On top was the dollar amount she hoped to invest.

"Holy crow!" Amber said.

Elise's eyes went wide. "Why do you live in this place when you have money like that?" Elise asked.

Nora chuckled. "I like to save," she said with a smile.

"Yet another reason why we can't let you invest. Now you'd be spending," Elise said.

Nora shook her head. "Investing. The complete opposite of spending. I love investing as well," she said. Her portfolio proved it.

"Mom, if this goes under, we'll feel badly. Terribly. But if your money sank along with all of our other investors' and our blood, sweat, and tears . . . I couldn't, we couldn't handle that," Amber said.

Elise nodded soundly as if that was the end of that.

"This is quite a bit of money, but I can afford to lose it," Nora said. Then she quickly added, "Not that I believe in the least that I'm going to lose it. I have full faith in you girls. Not only the two of you as people but also this venture. Are you really not going to let me be a part of it? I have full and complete confidence that I'll get back a high return on every dollar I invest. I've investigated this the same way I've checked out every one of my investments. It is sound. You two are sound. This is not an act of charity. This is me wanting to get in on the ground floor of something incredible," Nora said honestly.

The girls turned to one another, speaking in that nonverbal way only sisters can.

"Really?" Elise asked.

"Truly. I think this is an incredible opportunity. For me," Nora said.

Elise looked back at Amber, her eyes full of hope.

"With this kind of money, and as long as we get the loan we've applied for, we wouldn't need other investors," Amber stated honestly. "Would you be comfortable with that?"

"I would. But before you respond, read through my terms."

Nora pointed at the stack of papers. "You may not think I'm the best fit for your new company."

Elise scoffed, but Amber put a hand up. "She's right. Let's look this over," she said, sounding every bit the professional she was. Nora was so proud of her girls. And yet that truthfully wasn't the only reason she'd decided to invest.

Elise and Amber stood just as there was a knock on the front door.

"I'll get it," Nora offered since the girls were just about to go to the bedroom to read over her investment terms. Plus, it was her home after all.

Nora opened the door, her eyes going wide when she saw who was on the other side. She hadn't even realized Mack knew where she lived.

"Amber, Elise." Mack nodded toward the girls in greeting, the latter giggling as they returned the gesture.

"I wonder why he's here," Elise said much too loudly, Nora knowing full well that Mack had heard.

"Weren't you two about to go look over some paperwork?" Nora asked.

Amber nodded, but Elise was still laughing.

"You saw his face, right?" Elise asked as Amber shut the door behind them.

What about Mack's face? Nora looked back at the man waiting at her door and saw nothing out of the ordinary with the way he looked. Maybe his hair was a bit more ruffled, as if he'd been running his hand through it.

"Is everything okay at the gallery?" Nora asked.

Mack looked down the hall toward the stairs that led to the ground level of Nora's apartment building.

"Yeah, it's fine. I didn't work today," Mack said.

Nora raised a brow. She could've sworn Mack had been on the schedule.

"I switched my shift with Mary," Mack said, and Nora nodded. So the gallery was okay. Why wasn't he?

Now that Nora was watching him more carefully, something *was* out of place. Mack was breathing too hard, and he seemed too intense, unlike the easy-going man she knew. Wait, had he . . . had he slipped up?

She and Mack were both on sobriety journeys, and Nora knew how hard it was to stay clean even after all these years. Had something happened to Mack? A reminder of his sister who had passed when he was a teen? Or was it Kristie? Had something happened to the sweet girl they'd often visited when she'd been at the hospital during her chemo treatments?

"Mack, you're kind of scaring me. What's going on?" Nora asked as she held the door open.

"Can I come in?" Mack asked, pulling the collar of his green polo shirt away from his neck.

"Of course," Nora said, holding the door wider to let Mack in and then leading him to her couch.

"Nora," Mack said as they both sat.

She nodded. He needed to say something.

"I've never been more freaked out in my life," he said.

Nora wasn't sure what to say to that. Honestly, she was pretty freaked as well.

"I've tried to find the right words to say, but everything seemed wrong. All I know is that doing this is right," Mack said.

Nora was still lost.

"We need to go on a date, Nora. A real date. Not one I tricked you into, like at the hospital. I want you to get dressed up, and I want to come to your door. I want to take you to a nice restaurant and tell you how beautiful you are. I want to drive you home and worry about how I'll ask you on a second date because the first one was the best date of my life," Mack said.

Nora leaned back against her couch. There was so much to

process. Sure, Mack had asked her out before. But that was all part of the banter the two of them had going. This, on the other hand, didn't feel like banter.

"Mack . . ." Nora said, staring straight ahead.

But before responding, Mack took both of her hands in his, causing her to turn to him. "I know you're scared. Because you feel what I feel, right? This is real. What we have, if we explore it, would be real. The realest thing either of us have ever experienced. But we've both spent our whole lives running from real emotions. Running from real love," Mack said, hitting Nora's fears on the head.

When Nora gave up Amber for adoption, she promised she would never endure that same heartache again. And the only way to do that was by keeping everyone, especially good men, at arm's length. And there was no better man than Mack.

"I don't know," Nora finally said, unsure if her answer made any sense. But it was what she felt. She didn't know anything right now.

"I like you," Mack said as his grip on her hands tightened, telling her he'd never let go. Not as long as she wanted him.

"Tell me you don't like me," he said.

Nora was silent. She couldn't. She did like Mack. She'd tried to tell herself he was just a flirt, the kind of guy other women ended up with. He was too charming, too good looking, too everything for her.

"I like you," Nora whispered.

"We have to explore this, whatever is growing between us. We've both tried to ignore it, but I think it might eat me whole," Mack said.

Nora looked into his eyes to see determination mixed with desperation. Her stomach flipped. She knew what would happen if she said *no*. The same feeling Mack was now experiencing would consume her. She'd feel lost. She'd feel like she'd let go of something that she needed. Because she was beginning to believe she needed Mack. And she might even be ready for Mack in her life now that she'd found Amber. Now that she had a good relationship with her daughter.

"Please say *yes*," Mack whispered.

Nora fought against it. This would mean admitting that she'd fallen for Mack, because she had. This would mean giving Mack a chance to break her heart, because he could. And this would mean putting her fears aside and letting her heart rule, which scared her most of all. But even with all those reasons keeping her silent, Nora had to say it.

"Yes," she whispered back.

Mack's face transformed. Gone was the desperation, and his smile lit Nora from the inside out.

"Really?" he asked.

"Really," she said with a nod, feeling more determined with each passing second. She wouldn't run from Mack. Not anymore. Not when he'd laid himself on the line like this. Told her this was different for him as well.

"Okay," Mack said as he stood, bringing Nora with him.

They stood, their hands the only things keeping their bodies apart.

"I really want to kiss you," Mack said.

Nora realized she felt the same: an overwhelming urge to lift her mouth to meet Mack's lips.

"But I'm going to wait until our date," he added.

Nora almost sighed with disappointment. And yet the words thrilled her.

"Our date," Nora said, and Mack nodded.

"Are you free tomorrow evening?" he asked.

Nora laughed. This man didn't mess around. She worked in the morning, so she was free. She nodded.

"I'll pick you up at six," Mack said.

Nora nodded again. She was going on a date with Mack.

Oh man, he was going to look amazing. Not that he didn't right at this moment, but she could just imagine him all dressed up and . . . she was so done for.

Mack opened the door with grace Nora didn't possess in that moment and walked outside. "I need to leave or that kiss will happen right now," he said.

Nora understood. He wasn't the only one wishing away the minutes until the next evening.

"Good night, Nora," Mack said as he closed the door behind him.

Nora leaned against it, letting herself bask in the moment. She remembered Mack's disheveled hair with a smile. How long had he been debating before finally coming over? Her stomach flipped, and she worried. What if after this date she still felt what she did but Mack didn't? Nora swallowed, trying to summon her bravery. But she hadn't used it in a while. At least not in the dating arena. But this was what dating was. Putting herself out there. Seeing what came of things. And she knew one thing for sure: Mack was worth it.

Giggling and the sound of the bedroom door opening alerted Nora to the reentrance of her girls.

"Oh my gosh, that was the absolute sweetest thing I've ever heard," Elise declared as she put her hands to her heart. "That man is absolutely smitten."

Nora smiled. He kind of was.

"He really is flipped, Mom. But is he good enough for you?" Amber asked with her hands on her hips, acting the part of protective daughter to a T.

"He may be too good," Nora said honestly.

"Not possible, Mama Nora," Elise said as she pulled Amber with her across the room, and the two gave Nora a gigantic hug.

"So this is nice and all," Amber said from within the hug,

"but if that date is tomorrow, we'd better get moving on finding you the right outfit."

Elise pulled away immediately at those words and dragged both women by their hands to Nora's closet.

"Wait, did you go over the paperwork?" Nora asked as she noticed it still in Amber's hand.

"Are you kidding? We couldn't read and eavesdrop. Tomorrow, we deal with paperwork. Tonight, we ready you for your date with the most handsome man on the island," Elise said. and Nora couldn't disagree with that.

CHAPTER THIRTEEN

"THEY HATED ME," Alexis said to Jared over the phone, wishing they could have this talk in person. But their schedules were just too hectic. Jared had his kids much more than he typically did now that Marsha was back with her rich, married boyfriend. So Jared's days were consumed with getting his kids ready and off to school, work, and then helping his kids with homework, dinner, family time and bedtime. Alexis's life was quite busy as well, between the HIIT dance class she taught several mornings a week and then working at the food truck nearly every afternoon and evening. By the time the two of them were home, with kids in bed, they were too exhausted to talk, much less drive to see the other.

It had been nearly a week since their disastrous date, and this was the first time they were getting to talk. At least really talk. Each of their last four phone calls had been interrupted by Jared's kids, and once Margie had had a wedding emergency.

If Alexis weren't falling so hard for the man on the other end of the line, she would've given up. Because fighting for what they had was hard. Worth it but really hard. Especially because their biggest enemy in their fight to stay together was Jared's kids. No, that wasn't fair. They weren't the enemy, even if it felt that way since they were trying to keep Jared and Alexis apart. Not that Alexis could blame them. Their own mother was feeding them poison, and those poor kids were stuck in the middle.

"*Hate* is a strong word," Jared said.

Alexis imagined that he was sitting against his gray headboard in his mostly gray and black bedroom. Jared hadn't done much to change their home since Marsha had moved out—he just hadn't had the time—but he'd completely redecorated the master bedroom to the masculine colors they were now.

Alexis had only seen it once in passing. They weren't at the stage where they frequented each other's homes. In fact, they might never get there. And that thought depressed Alexis to her very core.

"But it's the right word," Alexis said, trying to keep her tone light even though it wasn't what she felt.

Jared laughed, the deep, soothing sound she needed to hear. If they could just see one another more, maybe this would work itself out. But between their schedules and the fact that his kids didn't want to see Alexis, they spent so much time apart that it didn't seem like the situation was going to change anytime soon.

But Alexis wasn't ready to give up.

"I miss you." Alexis breathed the words she was almost afraid to say. Did Jared feel the same way? Or was he starting to feel like what they were up against was too much to fight?

"Oh, I miss you so much," Jared returned, saying the words Alexis longed to hear. Good, maybe she wasn't the only one willing to work hard at this?

"I want to see you." Alexis sat up on her couch, feeling braver as she said those words.

"Then I'll come see you," Jared said, and Alexis heard rustling on the other end of the phone.

"Wait," Alexis said, trying hard not to imagine what Jared was doing within that rustling. She was guessing he was putting a shirt on his toned torso. Although Alexis had yet to see his bare chest, from the times she'd held him and touched him, Alexis knew what treasures lay below the surface, aka his shirt. "You can't leave the kids sleeping."

Jared groaned as if he'd just remembered his responsibility.

"Did you forget your kids?" Alexis asked with a chuckle.

"Am I a horrible person if I say that I did?" he asked in response, and Alexis laughed.

"I didn't exactly forget them. I just forgot I had them," Jared said.

"You mean the way you've had them for the past two weeks straight?" Alexis teased.

"I was a little distracted by a beautiful woman asking me to come over to her home," Jared said.

Alexis felt her stomach warm. "I could always come over there," she offered because she really wanted to see Jared, but then she remembered that wouldn't be easy either. What if the kids woke up and saw Alexis in their home? He hadn't said the words outright, but Alexis knew Jared didn't want to do anything to jeopardize the feeling of safety his kids had in his home. And Alexis would do that for them. At least right now.

"But I shouldn't," Alexis said so Jared didn't have to.

"It won't always be like this," he said, and Alexis wished she could believe that promise. But how did he know? His kids would hate her as long as Marsha wanted them to. Or until they were disillusioned with their mother, seeing her for the liar she truly was. And Alexis didn't wish that on those sweet children. Although they hadn't been so sweet to her, Alexis understood where their actions came from. The kind of hurt they'd endured. And she didn't want to do anything to add to that. The more she fell for Jared, the more she cared for those kids.

Alexis suddenly realized there was only one thing to do. Marsha was the only one who could change things. She and Jared could tell the kids the truth about their relationship and their mother, but that would hurt the kids. The best way to change things for the children was to talk to Marsha, no matter how painful it would be for Alexis. She had to try.

"I need to talk to Marsha," Alexis suddenly said, and she heard Jared's intake of breath.

"I'm not sure that's such a good idea," Jared responded warily.

Alexis smiled to herself when she realized that Jared was trying to protect her, something most of the men in her life hadn't done for her in the past. She was still getting used to the idea that a man who cared for her would try to keep her safe from all the scary things of the world . . . including Marsha. Alexis was grateful she'd taken so much time between dating Dalton, her cheating ex, and Jared or else she might've assumed that Jared was hiding something by keeping Alexis away from Marsha. But now with her baggage firmly stowed away where it belonged, Alexis could see Jared's true motives without her past clouding her view. Jared just wanted to protect her from the viciousness of Marsha.

"I'm a big girl," Alexis promised.

"I know that." Alexis heard Jared moving, telling her how uncomfortable he was with the situation. "But this is *my* fault, so it's my issue. I married her. Shouldn't I be the one to deal with her?"

Alexis had thought about that already. But at the beginning of this call, Jared had told Alexis that he'd tried, unsuccessfully, to mention to Marsha that her toxic words about Alexis were only serving to poison their children. To say that conversation hadn't gone well was an understatement. The fight that had ensued got Jared nowhere and only served to enrage Marsha more. Because Marsha and Jared had an explosive past. He already had to fight her on so much. On things that mattered more, like the situation with their children. Alexis didn't want to send Jared into battle again, not if she could take his place.

"Haven't you already tried?" Alexis asked.

"Yeah, but I could try harder," Jared said. "Make her see things my way."

Alexis chuckled, a dry sound that wasn't very full of humor. She was too sad to truly laugh.

"How's that worked for you in the past?" she asked, and she knew she had Jared. Not that she wanted to stump him, but his solution wasn't viable. At least not right now.

"Her words are hurting my kids," Jared said.

"I know," Alexis said, hating where Jared was in this situation. Wishing she could make it better for him. And she could try. Maybe Marsha would be so surprised by Alexis standing up to her that she would give in.

But honestly, Alexis didn't have much hope. Even if she spoke to Marsha, she doubted anything would change. But she had to try. She couldn't give up.

"She knows we're over," Jared said.

"I know," Alexis answered again.

"She wants us to be over. So why is she doing this? What's the point of asking our kids to hold on to a past that will never be?" Jared said the words Alexis had been thinking. What kind of woman could be so cruel to her own children? Someone too self-absorbed to care to see the truth.

"So you'll let me try to talk to her?" Alexis asked, not wanting to go above or around Jared on this. She needed them to be on the same page.

"I don't want to," Jared said. "I know she'll hurt you."

His last words came out in a protective growl, and Alexis loved him for that.

Wait, what? Oh no. Alexis didn't love this man, did she? It was hard enough to deal with this knowing she was *falling* in love, but already in love? She couldn't be, could she? It was too fast. Yet all the signs were there—

Alexis couldn't think about that now.

"I'll be fine. And I have to do this. For us," she said, hoping to let Jared know this was something she wasn't only willing but wanting to do. Jared had to understand she would sacrifice nearly anything to help them work. And she was so willing because she knew he would do exactly the same thing.

"If I were there right now, just know you'd be in my arms," Jared said softly.

"I know," Alexis said.

"If you want to back out—"

"I won't," Alexis interrupted. She was going to talk to Marsha. It was a matter of when, not if.

"You're my very own Wonder Woman, saving the day," Jared said.

That made Alexis laugh. "I'm no superhero," she said through her laughter.

"You are to me," Jared said softly, and Alexis's laughter stopped.

"Most likely nothing will come of this," Alexis said.

"I know. But you're going into the lion's den for me and my kids. You'll never know how much this means to me," Jared said, but Alexis could imagine. He'd already stood up to Marsha's wrath just by asking Alexis out. He wasn't the only one who'd put them in this position. Jared couldn't have chosen a woman who Marsha would hate him to be with more, thanks to Alexis's mother's relationship with Bill. Yet Jared had stuck with that decision. He'd stuck with Alexis.

And for that, Alexis was about to face her greatest foe. For better or worse.

ALEXIS DRUMMED her fingers on her steering wheel as she waited for those on the ferry to disembark. She and Jared had come up with a plan, the best way to approach Marsha with their plea. Jared thought they had at least a thirty percent chance of succeeding with this plan. Alexis thought he was optimistic. But so far, things had worked in their favor.

Bess had been happy to cover for Alexis that afternoon since Marsha would be coming in on the four-fifteen ferry. Marsha would be coming back from visiting her on-again boyfriend, so Jared guessed it would probably be the best time to find Marsha in good spirits. And, hopefully, she'd be willing to put her claws away. One could only hope.

Alexis had found an open parking spot right next to Marsha's car. So when Marsha headed for her car, Alexis wouldn't miss her. It did feel a bit like accosting the woman, but if anyone could handle a confrontation, it was Marsha. Besides, Alexis was ready with all the prettiest words to try to win Marsha to her side. Alexis had decided against calling Marsha *dragon woman* or any of the other nicknames she'd not-so-cleverly come up with. When two preteens hated you for the sole reason of their mother lying to them about you, it was hard not to console yourself by making up terrible nicknames.

But those thoughts were banished. Alexis was going to fight fire with kindness. And if that didn't work, well, Alexis would come to that if she had to.

Alexis's heart jumped as she saw the familiar figure of the woman who was challenging so many parts of her life. Because not only was Marsha messing things up for Alexis and Jared, she'd officially robbed Alexis of the opportunity to be at her mother's side for the most important event of Margie's life.

Alexis had gotten a call that very morning that her mother

and soon-to-be stepdad were going to elope. That afternoon. The intimate family wedding that they'd hoped to have just wouldn't be the same without Marsha or her children there. And since Marsha refused to have anything to do with Margie, Margie hoped that eloping would help her and Bill feel better about the family estrangement. If they got married with the rest of the family in tow, it would be too easy to notice that those three family members were missing. But if no one accompanied them and it was just Bill and Margie together—by romantic choice—Marsha's absence wouldn't mar their beautiful day.

Hearing the reason behind their choice, Alexis couldn't help but heartily approve of her mother and Bill's decision. She didn't blame them in the least, and she really hoped this elopement would help them to feel a stronger bond, something they could use to overcome future trials. Thanks to Marsha, more of them were sure to come their way.

But it didn't change the fact that Marsha's actions had forced Alexis to miss the wedding of her mother and best friend. So for that, and so much more, Alexis was beyond aggravated with the woman in a too-fancy-for-a-Friday-afternoon dress heading in her direction. *Marsha* was the reason Jared's kids hated her. *Marsha* was the reason why she and Jared might never be. And *Marsha* was also the reason why she wouldn't be at the only wedding her mother would ever have.

But all those thoughts of frustration had to go away. Alexis drew in what she hoped would be a calming breath. She was fighting fire with *kindness*. It was hard to remember because of the anger she'd left at a near boil on the back burner, but a more mature, less vindictive version of her had decided to take that path, and she was going to follow it. Even if the only person her kindness killed was herself.

Marsha was a few steps from her car, so it was time for Alexis to make her move. Alexis opened her car door, and the movement caught Marsha's attention. She hadn't been smiling before, but her look then had been vastly better than the scowl on her lips now.

"Alexis," Marsha said, as if she'd known Alexis would be waiting for her.

Dang it. Alexis had hoped the element of surprise would work in her favor. Count on Marsha to be cool and in control of every situation. So far, not so good.

"If you're here to plead your dreadful mother's case, don't. I don't care about her, and right now, my father has chosen her over me. So I don't care about him either," Marsha said flippantly. But even Alexis, who didn't know Marsha well, could see that she was lying. She might not give a flying fig about Margie, but Marsha did care about her father. It had been evident by the flash of pain in her eyes when she'd mentioned him. Meaning the woman had a heart. Hallelujah! Maybe Alexis's cause wasn't completely lost? She just had to go about this in the right way.

"I'm not here for my mom." Alexis thought about telling Marsha their parents were maybe getting married at that very moment. But that wasn't her news to share.

"Then it's about you. And my ex," Marsha muttered, as if she couldn't be bothered with the situation. "What is it with you women trying to take the men from my life?" Marsha added, this time more loudly.

So much was on the tip of Alexis's tongue. So much she could say about Marsha. But this wasn't going to go like that. Kindness. She was going to fight Marsha with kindness. So Alexis was going to point out reality in the nicest and kindest tone of voice possible.

"Jared isn't in your life anymore. By your choice." Alexis thought reminding Marsha that Jared hadn't been hers long before Alexis ever came along was necessary before they could move on. Marsha had to understand that very simple fact.

"He's the father of my children. He will always be in my life," Marsha said.

Alexis had to nod at that. Marsha had a point, and not just on her extra-long fingernails.

"But why tell those children that I'm the one keeping your family apart?" Alexis asked, hoping the sweetness in her voice wasn't overdoing it. But Alexis felt her anger creeping in, and she had to keep it at bay.

"Because it's the truth," Marsha said with a raise of her hands as if the answer was obvious.

Deep breath. In and out. Alexis wasn't sure she was going to survive this. How was that the truth? Only in a fantasy world could Alexis be the one tearing Jared's family apart. Their family had been broken. Long before Alexis. By Marsha. Alexis tried to rein in her frustration before she spoke again. She needed Marsha to see reality. And hopefully telling her the truth kindly would do it. Because Alexis had no other strategy.

"No. It's not. You left Jared. You're dating someone else. Why shouldn't Jared do the same?" Alexis asked, trying to keep her voice level. She wasn't exactly being kind anymore, but she couldn't allow herself to show her anger.

"Nolan is in Seattle. With his own family. If Jared dates you, you will be here. With no one. Nolan does nothing to threaten our family unit. You do," Marsha said, as if it were the most logical thing in the world.

"What?" Alexis sputtered, completely flabbergasted. Did Marsha really think that as long as the kids didn't see they were dating other people, they could pretend to be a family?

"Would you be okay with Jared dating a married woman in Seattle?" Alexis asked. She hadn't meant the words to be an arrow, but judging by the way Marsha straightened her shoulders, Alexis had hit her mark. And the battle had begun.

Dang it! Alexis hadn't wanted to do that.

"I think we're through here," Marsha said, and Alexis knew she only had moments left.

"Your kids are confused, Marsha. They think you'll be a family again as long as I'm out of the picture," Alexis pleaded. "That isn't fair to them."

"It is if it's the truth," Marsha said as she walked closer to her car.

What?!

"You would go back to Jared if I wasn't in the picture?" Alexis asked, needing Marsha to hear how ridiculous her words were.

"I'd go back to the way we were when we were a family," Marsha said as she opened her car door.

"You mean you'd go back to living in his house while cheating on him?" Alexis asked, her eyes going wide in shock. She couldn't truly mean that, could she?

Marsha shot Alexis a blank look telling Alexis that was exactly what she was planning.

"He'd never take you back!" Alexis shouted.

"You underestimate what Jared will do for his children," Marsha said before getting in the car and slamming the door shut, effectively cutting off all communication.

No! Alexis wanted to shout, but Marsha peeled out of her parking space and was gone. Alexis's chance was gone. Marsha was going to change nothing. And although Alexis had been pretty sure this was how their conversation would end, she had to admit that that last string of hope that she could maybe get Marsha to change had really kept her going.

But it hadn't happened. At all. If anything, Marsha had dug her red heels in even further.

What could Alexis do now? Especially because Marsha wanted Jared back, in the most twisted way. But was she right? Would Jared go back to their fake marriage just for his kids? If anyone was selfless enough to do so, it was Jared. Would Alexis let him? Then again, could she stop him?

Alexis sank into her car seat and felt the tears stinging against her eyes. She thought about fighting them, but she was too tired. She gave in, and they began to roll down her cheeks followed by sobs. She loved Jared. She couldn't give him up. And yet she would. If it was best for him.

The chime of Alexis's text tone went off, and she was going to ignore it when she caught sight of the message from the corner of her eye. She saw a picture.

She opened her phone to investigate, and it was her mom and Bill. Kissing. Her mom's short, white veil framed her beautiful face, and their smiles, too large for life, couldn't be hidden. Alexis could see their grins, even around the kiss they were sharing. Her mom was married.

Alexis allowed a few more tears because she'd missed that moment. But she was thrilled for her mom and Bill. They'd gotten down the aisle. They'd fought for the other, fought together, and they'd won. Their struggles were far from over, but they were proving they could make it. They were going to make it. And that thought gave Alexis a tiny, new tendril of hope. Maybe she'd lost this battle, but if Jared was really on her side, could they make it? Maybe. She wasn't sure. But she did know she wasn't done trying. If her mom and Bill could overcome, so could she and Jared. And so far, Jared had proven he was completely on her side. Alexis would take that knowledge and move forward. Because she had to.

CHAPTER FOURTEEN

"THEY CAUGHT HIM?" Julia asked her security officer, needing him to reiterate what he'd just said.

"He caught him, ma'am," Dan, the newest member of her security team, said, and Julia fell back against Dax and Bess's couch with a sigh of relief. Her nightmare was over. Her stalker was in police custody. And Liam could leave.

"Oh, thank goodness," Bess breathed as Dax put an arm around Julia, being right beside her the way family should.

"Are you okay?" Dax asked Julia.

She nodded and then smiled at Bess. She really was grateful for all they'd done to support her. She didn't know what she would've done without her Whisling family or Ellis.

Oh my goodness . . . Ellis. She had to tell him the news immediately, even if he was about to get on stage in less than an hour. Yes, she now had Ellis's tour schedule memorized. No, she wasn't ashamed. Okay, maybe a bit embarrassed. But Ellis knew, and he thought she was adorable—his words, not Julia's.

Julia pulled out her phone to text the incredible news to the man she was falling for more and more every day. She wasn't sure who would be more thrilled by this turn of events, her or Ellis. And heaven knew she was ecstatic.

She sent off a quick text, not wanting to bother Ellis while he was in the middle of preconcert mania, but her phone began ringing immediately, and Julia laughed as she saw Ellis's number.

"Hello?" she said, her entire demeanor feeling lighter than it had in a month.

"Really?" Ellis asked, his voice offering Julia comfort even when she didn't need it.

"Really," Julia said, and Ellis let out a yelp any cowboy would be proud of.

"Put Dan on the line," Ellis said, and Julia laughed.

"You don't trust me?" Julia asked with mock outrage.

"Oh, I trust you, Darlin'. But I just want to make sure the next steps are all good and proper. I need Dan to take care of you until I can have you in my arms again." Ellis was taking the same care for her he'd been taking for the past couple of weeks. Julia's heart still flipped at the idea that after his tour, Ellis was coming home to her.

Julia handed the phone off to Dan, who she'd requested her security company send about a week before when she'd begun to worry if Liam would see her through to the end of this ordeal.

Liam.

In the beginning, the man had been exactly who Julia needed: a fresh face amidst the turmoil. But after a few days, it was easy to see he was starting to get antsy. Waiting for a stalker to strike took patience. And Liam quickly lost what little he had. It didn't take long after that for Julia to see what high school Julia and actress Julia never could. Liam wasn't built to stick around. Julia couldn't change that. She wondered if anyone could. Thankfully, she'd come to a point where she didn't wonder enough to need to find out. She was happy to let Liam go. As soon as her stalker was dealt with.

But with Liam getting an itch to move on—he was always distracted by his need to find some action—Julia had to turn to others for calm reassurance. Which Ellis, sweet and nearly perfect Ellis, gave her from afar. She'd also received lifelines of help from Bess, Alexis, Dax, Olivia, Deb, Nora, the list could go on with her Whisling friends who'd stepped up to the plate as Liam had backed away. It wasn't his fault, necessarily. Liam wasn't built for long-term.

But it had been three long weeks with no word from the stalker. Probably two and a half weeks too long, in Liam's book.

So it wasn't at all surprising when Liam took things into his own hands. He'd realized the stalker had struck while Julia was at a well-publicized event. From what they could tell, the stalker didn't know Julia personally but seemed in tune with the Whisling gossip network. So they'd used that. Told anyone who could possibly care that Julia would be going to a wedding planning event for Olivia and Dean that afternoon at Dax and Bess's home. Julia had let it "slip" that her security would be with her and not at her home. A completely empty house? Liam had hoped the situation would be too appealing for the stalker to pass up. And it had been.

"I'm sorry that we had to use your wedding planning as an alibi," Julia said when she realized she'd been in her thoughts for too long and was still within a group of people. A group of people who deserved gratitude for what they'd done for her.

Olivia grinned in response. "It was actually pretty exciting. I mean, I'm sure it was terrible for you, but for us . . ." Olivia clamped her mouth shut. She still hadn't quite gotten over being starstruck when it came to Julia. Sometimes she was completely fine, but other moments she tended not to say things eloquently as she typically would.

"What I think my lovely bride was trying to say is this is a welcome reprieve from all the typical wedding planning stuff. Although we'll just be having a simple ceremony with close friends and family, the planning is driving us up the wall. It's nice to be doing something different for a change. Even if the circumstances aren't so pleasant," Dean, ever the articulate lawyer, said for his wife, and she beamed up at her hero. They truly were perfect for each other.

Julia glanced away from the couple when she felt a tap on her shoulder, and Dan handed her back her phone. "Mr. Rider said, and I quote, 'My manager is going to have my behind if I don't get on stage immediately.' So he'll call you after his show tonight."

Julia grinned like a silly school girl at the words Dan had relayed. But Ellis did that to her. She couldn't help it.

"And we really should go" Dan suggested not-so-subtly.

Julia looked from her hosts to her other friends. "I'm sorry we don't have more time to talk about the big event, but evidently I'm needed back at home," Julia said.

Olivia waved her away. "Of course. That was the point of all this. But you'll come to the wedding, won't you?" Olivia asked.

Julia nodded. She wouldn't miss the wedding between these two lovebirds for the world.

"Thank you again for the safe haven," she said to Bess and Dax, who both smiled in response.

"We wouldn't have wanted you to go anywhere else. You always have a place with us," Bess said.

Julia couldn't believe how welcoming the woman was. She deserved her beautiful life and so much more.

Julia grinned at her friends, showing them she was relieved at the way the afternoon had gone.

But as soon as she began following Dan toward the door, she knew the time for smiles had passed. This was serious business.

She'd need to get together with her security team and the police. Find out who this stalker was. What he wanted. How she could keep him from ever coming into her home again.

Julia loved that even though she'd been scared by her stalker, in this moment she felt empowered, ready to take her life back.

"Is there anything else I need to know before I get home?" Julia asked as she got into the car that Dan had driven to Bess's home.

Dan shook his head. "Liam asked that he be the one to apprise you of the situation," Dan responded authoritatively but kindly.

Julia nodded, knowing Dan had told her all she needed to know. In the week she'd known him, Dan never left her in the dark. Unlike Stan. Also, this security officer said more than a word to her at a time. He was actually the kind of guard she could see having around for the long haul.

With nothing left for Dan to tell her, Julia's thoughts ran wild with all that was coming next as they drove the short distance to her home. She knew now that the stalker had been caught, she'd be having a security shake up. One that needed to happen for Liam's sake. She had to let him go. In every way. Once and for all. And interestingly enough, she wasn't the least bit sad about it. Letting Liam go felt so right.

For years, Julia had wondered "what if" when it came to Liam. What if they were given a second chance? What if they were in the same place long enough for the two to get to know one another? What if they were meant to be?

Julia now had the answers to those questions and so many more. With time together, Liam would annoy the heck out of her. The man, although a military man at some point in his life, was now a slob. And Julia loved her neat and tidy way of life. He also slurped his soup and liked to listen to hard rock at all hours of the day. He was a whirlwind when all Julia wanted was calm. Liam had been in one place for quite a while, and it had nearly driven him crazy. Liam craved change the way Julia craved stability. He'd never be satisfied with Julia, and Julia came to realize she wouldn't be satisfied with him either. They were definitely not meant to be. And that thought had Julia feeling even lighter than before.

As they got within sight of her home, Julia let all thoughts of Liam go once and for all. They'd deal with the remnants of the stalker, and then Liam would move on.

Julia's eyes spied three police cars in her driveway, and with that sight, her heart sped up. Was her stalker still here? Would she have to see him? She hoped to heaven not, but she wasn't sure. Was this part of why she'd had to come back? Did they want to see if Julia recognized him? Julia realized that although she wasn't thrilled at that prospect, she wasn't exactly terrified either.

Because now that this was all over, she was beginning to realize that she'd never been in true fear for her life because of this stalker. She'd hated that he had invaded her home, bypassed her security. But, and maybe this was naive on her part, she'd never felt like this stalker wanted to harm her. He'd chosen a time when she wasn't around to leave that rose. And then he'd stayed away. Then again, Julia had heard enough stories where these kinds of things escalated quickly—it was hardly ever stable people who became stalkers. So even though she wasn't petrified by the stalker, she didn't want to meet him either.

Sometime after arriving in her driveway, Julia had slunk down in her seat so that she wasn't visible above the window. Julia peeked up over the edge as Dan drove her past each of the police cars. Thankfully, they were empty. The stalker must've been taken to the station already.

Julia breathed a sigh of relief as Dan stopped in front of the house. The front door burst open, and a very alive-looking Liam came striding down the front steps. From the smile on his lips to the way he nearly glided down the stairs, Julia could see Liam was a lot happier than he had been in a long time. All of Julia's aforementioned suspicions were confirmed with just one look. Liam had to live on the edge of danger or he just couldn't be content.

Liam opened her car door and pulled her into his arms. Gone were the days her heart would flutter at his touch. It now felt like hugging her brother, Jack, or Dax.. She was sure Liam would hate to be clumped in with that group—she'd learned the man loved being wanted, probably another reason why he'd entered Julia's life every fifteen years—but friendship was now all she felt for him. And on Julia's part, she felt nothing but peace about that revelation.

"You're safe," Liam promised.

Julia nodded. Thank goodness.

"Do you know a Peter Andrews?" Liam asked.

Julia shook her head. The name didn't ring any bells.

"We didn't think you would. He's a longtime resident of Seattle. We've done a quick background search, and it doesn't seem like your paths intersected at any time," Liam said.

Julia nodded, loving that she was finally getting answers.

"Why was he on Whisling?" Julia asked.

Liam raised an eyebrow. He was here for her. Julia felt a knot tighten in her stomach.

"I'm only telling you this information so that you can make the smartest decision as far as future security," Liam said, making it clear that he wanted to be off the island as much as Julia wanted him to leave. She was grateful they were on the same page. There was nothing wrong with the man. He'd become a friend. It's just that he was driving her insane.

But Liam leaving meant Julia was vulnerable again. She

thought back to the way she'd felt when Stan had been her security officer—how utterly alone she'd been. Because even though he'd been sent to watch over her, he hadn't thought of her as a real person. And that was something she needed. Especially if she ever had to endure a stalker again.

Having a stalker had been one of Julia's greatest fears throughout her career. She'd had friends who'd endured the same, actually a few of them much worse, and she'd prayed that her day would never come. However, it had. And Julia realized that even though it had been terrible to live through—she'd be wary of another stalker for years to come—the worst had happened and she had gotten through it. She was now a woman who could overcome one of her greatest fears . . . with the help of her friends.

That thought gave her hope as she finally decided how she wanted to deal with her lack of security. One thing this stalker had taught her was that she no longer wanted to live completely alone. And in the last couple of days, Julia had learned to appreciate Dan. He wasn't quite the friend Liam was, but he was a calming presence, and he seemed at home on the island. Which wasn't surprising, considering he'd been born and raised on an island in the Pacific. And heaven knew he was much neater than Liam could ever be. Julia might even offer to hire Dan privately. Even though she liked her security company, it would be nice to have her bodyguard answer to her and only her.

"Thanks, Liam," Julia finally said after her thoughts had run their course. Now that she knew what she wanted to do, she felt like she could really let Liam go.

"That *thank you* kind of sounded like goodbye," Liam said with a slight smile.

"It was," Julia said. "You've been chomping at the bit for days now."

Liam grimaced. "Have I been that bad?"

"Snapping at me for trying to make you pancakes, and then muttering *where in the hell is that stalker?* Nope, not too bad," Julia said with a laugh, hoping to lighten the words. Liam just wasn't made for domesticated life.

Liam nodded. "Sounds like me. You know, Julia, I always wondered if our stars would align," he said.

Julia felt her stomach drop. Liam didn't actually think, after all this, that they could work out, did he?

"And they finally did," he said in a tone that told Julia he wasn't pining for her in the least. She could now tell where this was going, and it was good. They were good.

"And we get to part as friends. Better than any torrid love affair," Julia said with a grin.

Liam raised an eyebrow. "Are you sure about that?"

Julia laughed at his response, swatting him the way she would with any friend. She would never wish a stalker on anyone, but at least this experience had brought her closure with Liam. She would never wonder *what if* again.

"Ms. Price." One of the police officers came out of her home and joined Julia and Liam on her front porch. Julia realized she'd been avoiding going inside. She wasn't quite prepared to see the mess the stalker had left behind.

"I just spoke to the arresting officer who has had a conversation with the suspect," the officer said, and Julia nodded.

"Sounds like the guy is willing to get some psychiatric help," the officer said with a smile. "That's a good thing, Ms. Price."

Julia nodded again. It was. Hopefully with some mental help, this man would never be after her again.

"Another good thing is that he never entered your home while you were in it. I used to work in the city, and lots of these cases don't end up like this. But even though it turned out better than most, we'll still be letting you know when and for how long the suspect will be incarcerated. You'll know what happens every step of the way. However, I just wanted to let you know, despite how this seems, I think you're one of the lucky ones."

Julia leaned back against the wall next to her front door. Those weren't words she'd been expecting. But then again, they were true. Considering all that could've happened, she was a lucky one.

"We'll be out of your hair in a minute, and you'll be able to get your home back. Fortunately, since your bodyguard stopped the suspect before he entered your home, you should have little to no mess to clean up."

"Stopped him before he came inside?" Julia asked, her voice going up with her question.

"As soon as he breached your property, ma'am. We've been in the backyard. That's where the altercation took place," the officer said before leaving the porch and going back through the house to the backyard to gather his colleagues.

"You kept him out of my house?" Julia asked, turning back to Liam with a face full of gratitude.

"I did my best. Turned out, my best worked," Liam said with a grin. Then he added more somberly, "I saw how that first crime scene messed with you. I wanted to help you get your home back."

Julia stepped forward, wrapping her arms around her friend.

"Thank you. Truly, thank you," she said.

"If I get a hug like that every time I save you, I might have to save you more often," Liam said.

"My hope is never again," Julia said with a sigh.

"Really? I thought it was kind of fun," Liam admitted.

Julia shook her head. "You were made for a life of adventure. I was made for a life of quiet retirement," she responded as she pulled away from the hug, and Liam laughed.

The officers began to stream toward their cars, some coming

through the front door and a couple coming around the side of the house from the backyard. It was quite a few police officers, but then again, Whisling didn't often see much crime. Julia wondered if this had been as exciting of an afternoon for them as it had been for Liam.

"So goodbye?" Liam asked as he put out his hand for Julia to shake. She shook it and then nodded.

For whatever reason, she was sure this was the last time she'd be seeing Liam. He'd played a weirdly vital role every fifteen years, but now it was time to really say *adieu*. He didn't need her and she, for the first time, could honestly say she no longer needed him.

"Visit home more often. They could use seeing more of you," Liam said as he walked toward his rental car. Not surprisingly, it was already packed. Liam had known his time was up too.

"I will," Julia promised because going home more often was what she needed as well.

"I hope you find what you're looking for," Julia said as Liam closed the car door. She was sure he hadn't heard her, but then he met her eye and winked. She really did hope the best for him.

Julia turned back to the house before Liam could drive away. She didn't want to watch him leave her life because, even though she didn't need him, it didn't mean she wouldn't miss him.

She looked up at her home and finally found comfort in the brick and mortar again, something that had been missing since the stalker first appeared. She'd loved her piece of paradise, and Liam had given her back that love.

But it was time to move on and find Dan. She had a job to offer.

CHAPTER FIFTEEN

BESS BURROWED DEEPER into her thick winter coat and her husband's side. She loved calling Dax her husband. She and Dax were in the first of the five rows of chairs set out on the beach that she knew held a special place in Olivia's and Dean's hearts. It was the place where they'd been reacquainted after years apart. It was the place where Olivia had begun to find herself after the years of abuse she'd endured at the hands of Bart. It was the place of new beginnings for the two of them and, therefore, the perfect place for them to start their new life together.

But it was a chilly place to decide to get married in the middle of December. Fortunately, the temperatures were warm for a winter day, and they'd arranged for their outdoor vows to take place at one in the afternoon when there'd be the least chance of rain and the most chance of heat. But Bess was still grateful that there was a portable heater not even two feet from her.

Bess glanced over at her misty-eyed in-laws gazing up at their beautiful daughter as she said *I do* to the man of her dreams.

Olivia looked absolutely radiant and a little cold in her midnight blue wedding dress. It was a bit of a leap from the traditional white, but Olivia hadn't wanted to wear white again. She didn't want to replicate the dress from her first wedding in any way, shape or form. This marriage would be so different, and she needed the wedding to reflect that.

So she wore blue, Dean's favorite color and the color of the sea right next to them. The long-sleeved dress that went into a deep v at the neck was embellished with silver threading along the bodice. Between her hair, which was pulled loosely back in a chignon, and the full skirt of the dress, Olivia looked every part the princess who'd finally found her prince.

Bess's eyes began to mist up as well. Her sweet friend and sister had been through hell and back, and she deserved every bit of her "happily ever after."

Olivia's gorgeous daughters stood as bridesmaids, each in mini versions of Olivia's dress. They weren't exactly matching, but the cohesive look was going to give the family photos a majestic grandeur that Bess was sure would be appreciated for years to come.

Pearl and Rachel beamed up at their soon-to-be stepdad and their mom, each moment their smiles seeming to widen somehow.

The other little girls in the wedding party weren't behaving quite as well as the bridesmaids, and Bess smiled as she watched her sister, Gen, step out from the row behind her to grab her sweet, little daughters who looked angelic in their silver flower girl dresses. But they weren't acting very angelic. Evidently Maddie had taken her sister's basket and squabbles had broken out.

Gen shot a look of apology at Olivia who just beamed back in response. Bess was pretty sure nothing could get to Olivia today.

As the minister continued with the ceremony, Bess caught movement out of the corner of her eye. Piper was moving to get a better shot of the couple.

Bess didn't know Piper well, but from what Deb and Nora had told her, the woman was holding up incredibly well even though she was facing every parents' very worst nightmare. According to Nora, Piper was able to lean on Kristie's dad, even though the two had been divorced for some years now. Nora also shared that Kristie was hopeful the two would get back together. But didn't every child of divorce hold on to that hope? Although Bess realized Kristie's hope was more poignant than other children since Kristie knew she would be leaving her parents soon. Nora had told Bess that Kristie's hope was because she didn't want to leave either of her parents alone. Bess couldn't imagine the kind of heart that had to reside in a teen so intent on looking out for those around her while she endured the worst. Bess realized she needed to reach out and get to know Piper. She was sure the woman would be able to use as many friends as possible in the coming days.

Dean's voice pulled Bess's attention back to the ceremony. He was repeating the vows the minister was saying. The happy couple had decided against writing their own vows. Olivia had said the words had worked for thousands of years before them, so why change a good thing? Dean had just been relieved to tick another thing off his wedding to-do list.

And the words really were beautiful as they promised to hold one another forever in front of God and all the people they loved.

Olivia began to repeat the same vows. "For richer or poorer," Olivia said, grinning through her words. She seemed too cheerful to take any of the words too seriously. "In sickness or in health. To love and to . . ." Olivia paused, moisture suddenly filling her eyes as she took in the man beside her. The man who was already cherishing her above all else.

"Cherish," she finally choked out as she squeezed Dean's hands. He nodded, and Bess knew something was passing between them. Something beautiful and only for them.

Olivia somehow managed the rest of her vows without breaking out again in the tears that threatened, and soon the couple was embracing and finally experiencing their first kiss as man and wife.

Dean deepened the kiss, causing the small gathering to erupt in cheers. Although, Olivia's dad did say loud enough for all to hear, "Thank goodness they didn't get married in a church."

Dax laughed at his dad's reaction, and Bess kept right on cheering. If anyone deserved a kiss like that, it was Olivia and Dean. They'd worked hard to not show too much PDA in front of both their families. But now they were married, and everyone could deal with it.

The couple rushed down the aisle, hand in hand, and back up to Dean's home, where a small reception would take place.

Bess breathed a sigh of relief that she didn't have to hurry up to the house behind them, even though she was in charge of the food for the small reception. Once again, Alexis had insisted she be the one to handle the actual event since it was Bess's sister-in-law's wedding. Bess had argued that Alexis was Olivia's friend as well, but Alexis had then countered that family trumped friendship. Bess didn't have a response to that argument.

Bess grinned at friends and family as they followed the couple down the aisle and up the beach toward the house as her thoughts turned back to Alexis. Bess was worried about her friend. The poor woman had finally found pure bliss with a good man, but there were still so many hurdles to jump. The last time Bess had spoken with Alexis, she'd said that Jared had promised they'd find a way for their relationship to triumph, even though his children were against them. But Bess was still concerned. She knew Alexis was worried as well. For now, all Alexis could do was hope for change. Bess was hopeful as well. And at least, according to what Bess had heard, Marsha was now finally taking her turn with their children. So Jared and Alexis had been able to go on a few consistent dates, just the two of them. They'd decided they'd focus on their relationship for the time being and try to win the kids over bit by bit.

"Who would've thought this day would come?" Dax's father's voice interrupted Bess's thoughts.

"What day?" Dax asked warily, the tone of his voice telling Bess he was pretty sure he was walking into a trap.

"The day we no longer have to worry about either of our kids," his father answered with a chuckle, earning himself a smack from Dax's mom, Kathryn.

"What your father meant to say was the day we see both of our children so very happily in love with partners who wholly deserve them," Kathryn said with a smile.

Dax's father added, "Yeah, what she said," which earned him another smack. He yelped in indignation before Kathryn yanked on his arm, pulling him toward the house.

"I swear I can't take you anywhere," Kathryn muttered, and Bess smiled. She knew their teasing was all good-natured. Dax's parents adored one another.

The Penns were followed by Lily, her husband, Allen, and their little Amelia. Lily was pushing Allen's wheelchair up the small hill that led to Dean's backyard while Amelia walked along next to them. Bess wasn't sure how they'd maneuvered the wheelchair down to the beach, but judging by their smiles and laughter, they hadn't been upset about the task.

"So they're married," Julia sighed as she took Bess's arm, and the two of them began their way up the aisle. If someone had told Bess the year before that she'd be friends with one of the biggest movie stars of their time, Bess would've laughed in their face. Yet, there she stood. Arm in arm with Julia and loving every minute of it. Julia had proved to be one of the very best people Bess had ever met: loyal, kind and a bit self-deprecating. That last part made her less intimidating than she would've been otherwise.

"Finally," Bess and Julia said in unison, and they both giggled.

"How are you doing?" Bess asked Julia. The last she'd seen of her, Julia had hurried out of Bess's home with news that her stalker had been caught.

"Great, actually," Julia said, and Bess looked at her friend to judge her honesty. Julia's face was full of sincerity, so Bess didn't call her friend out for lying. But really? Great? That seemed incredible considering the nightmare she'd endured.

"Did Liam leave?" Bess asked. Most recently, she'd heard that Julia was going to ask her friend to leave the island since his job was done, but Bess knew Julia was going to miss the man who'd once been the object of her desire.

"He did."

"And?" Bess asked.

"I miss him. Or more the part he played in my life. I guess as an actress I've cast people in roles, even if sometimes they didn't quite fit the part. I cast Liam as my great love, but he was never meant to play that role," Julia said with a shrug.

"And who was meant to play that role?" Bess asked cheekily.

Julia laughed softly. "Casting is still out on that one. If such a role exists," she said, and Bess pulled her friend into a side hug. Julia wasn't as slight as she used to be, but she was still smaller than most women Bess knew.

"The role is there. Just waiting," Bess promised.

"I wish I was as sure as you. Sometimes I think I had my

great love. Acting. Now that love has been laid to rest," Julia said as she pulled away from Bess.

Bess shook her head. She didn't believe that for her friend. "I know there's a really handsome country singer looking for a gig now that his world tour is almost complete," Bess teased.

Julia laughed. "If anyone was meant to play a hero, it's Ellis. I don't doubt that. I just doubt myself as the heroine." Julia added the last part quietly, and Bess decided she'd pried enough for one day.

Julia must've thought the same because she moved their conversation right along. "Did you hear Nora's girls got the property?" she asked.

"I did," Bess said with a gigantic grin. The property in question was going take a lot of work, but Bess was pretty sure if anyone could take it on, it was Nora's girls. They were young, ambitious, and determined. Bess couldn't wait to see what they would make of it. "Evidently, they moved onto the property full time in a trailer? They want to be on hand for every moment," Bess added.

Julia laughed. "Man, to be young and willing to live in a trailer for your dream," she said. "Then again, I did worse for mine."

"I can imagine. Your dream was a big one," Bess replied.

Julia nodded, her thoughts on times past. "And how is married life treating you?" she asked.

Bess felt her cheeks go pink. "Superbly," she said with a sigh.

"I'm glad to hear that," Dax said, his voice still causing a tingle up her spine. Married life hadn't stopped that little phenomenon.

His arm went around her waist, and he pulled her in close as they walked through Dean's backyard.

Julia looked from Bess to Dax and then around at their

surroundings as if looking for some kind of escape. Her eyes landed on her bodyguard.

"I think I see Dan over there. Probably needing some kind of direction. I'll leave you two," Julia said, and then she winked at Bess before walking toward where Dan stood just outside of the house.

"So, Mrs. Penn," Dax said as he stopped and pulled Bess into his arms. Since they'd waited for most of the guests to go up to the house before them and it was quite a chilly day, they were completely alone in the backyard.

"Yes, Mr. Penn?" Bess asked, her voice full of flirtation.

"Could you enjoy that wedding after the perfection of ours? I'm worried that our day has ruined you for all others. I mean, how could poor Olivia's compare?" Dax asked.

Bess let out a hearty laugh, but she quieted as she reflected on what Dax had said. His words had all been teasing, but there was some truth to what he'd said. Except Bess felt the exact opposite.

"Our wedding opened my eyes to the beauty of other weddings. I think now I can appreciate each nuance all the more because ours was exactly what I wished it would be. But more importantly, our marriage has opened my eyes to be able to see, feel, and experience the very best life has to offer. Because you, Dax Penn, have offered it to me," Bess said. Then she looked up at her husband as he gazed down on her.

"I was not expecting that," he said, his voice full of emotion. "You've done the same for me, Bess Penn."

Bess grinned as she felt Dax's grip on her waist tighten, and he captured her lips.

Life might not always be perfect on Whisling, but some moments were. Absolutely, deliciously perfect.

Made in United States
Orlando, FL
08 February 2022

14613103R00115